Why the Long Face?

Cover art by Laura Davidson, used by permission of the artist
Cover design by Kroner Design, Cambridge, MA

Printed in the United States

LIBRARY OF CONGRESS CATALOGING-IN-PUBLICATION
DATA
Ron MacLean, 1958
    Why the Long Face? / Ron MacLean – 1st American ed.
        ISBN 978-0-9744288-5-7

Swank Books
P.O. Box 300163
Jamaica Plain, MA 02130

Why the Long Face?

stories by Ron MacLean

Happy Birthday Amika!
Ya are a saint!
8·6·16

SWANK
BOOKS

Thanks to the editors of the following publications, where some of these stories first appeared:
"Last Seen, Hank's Grille" and "Las Vegas Wedding" in *Night Train*;
"The Encyclopedia of (Almost) all the Knowledge in the World" as "What Liebniz Didn't Know" in *The Little Magazine*;
"South of Why" in *GQ*;
"Mile Marker 283" in *Other Voices*;
"Aerialist" in *Sonora Review*;
"Where Morning Finds You" in *Reed*;
"Why I'm Laughing" in *Greensboro Rreview*;
"Over the Falls" in *Fear Not*, from Crawlspace Press

Aerialist

THE NIGHT OF THE FALL EQUINOX I walked into the living room to find my daughter standing suspended above the ground, arms out from her sides, eyes locked in concentration, bare legs flexed, ballet slipper-clad feet poised, one in front of the other, on a wrought iron curtain rod propped between couch and coffee table.

Katie has always had a tremendous sense of balance. When she was three months old, she could push herself to her feet, holding tight to my fingers, to her mother's fingers, and rock there, flexing leg muscles that even then longed to assert themselves. Ever since she could walk, she's been fascinated with moving on the edges of things, balancing, arms out, concentration furrowing her brow.

But I wasn't prepared for this: my five-year-old hovering two feet off the living room floor, walking across a rod as if it were an earth-bound curbstone.

"Katie," I said, ignoring the pork and vegetables that were in danger of burning. "How did you do that?" My eyes locked on hers. My body ready to pounce at the slightest hint of a fall.

The coy Katie grin, the one where she knows she's on to something, danced across her lips, but she said nothing.

"Little bird," I said. "How long have you been able to do this?"

Katie paused in her trek through the firmament of our living room, and placed an index finger on her lips.

"Shh, Dad," she said. "I'm practicing."

Sometimes you have to give yourself over to mystery. I tried to accept this as something Katie could do. Some children have a knack for Legos, some for puzzles. My wife Monica, when she was alive, had double-jointed elbows. Katie could walk on air.

I tried to remain rooted in practicalities. Logistics. How had she moved the curtain rod from behind the couch? I'd forgotten it was there, after months of intending to install it. How had she hoisted the heavy wrought iron? How had it occurred to her? These questions I could handle. They had potential answers. Other questions terrified me – *how – where – had my child learned this?*

One fall day, just at the time Monica got sick, the sky an angry silver, air turning cold, Katie at three, climbing to the observation deck at Blue Hills. Scrambling her way up this mountain, keeping up, my brother-in-law Joel and I experienced hikers. I kept waiting for Katie to give up, to ask to be carried. But she climbed, clawed, strode her way up, purposeful. At the summit, we stood on flat rock, looking out over Greater Boston, all three of us hands on hips. The amazement in Katie's blue eyes. Her ability to command this view. We couldn't get her to leave. She stood on an outcrop, leaned into the wind, unconcerned by the void below. I had to pull her back, kicking and screaming, vertigo dizzying me as I looked down. But this isn't the sort of thing that makes you conclude that your daughter is going to be an aerialist.

Some people would call me a recluse since Monica died. I don't get out much. Moved my business home. Rarely meet clients. But here's how I see it. Katie's all I've got left, and it takes everything I have to protect her.

"What does the future hold for her," I asked Monica one evening as we warmed ourselves with tea. Nightly tea after putting Katie to bed is a ritual we've continued since Monica's death a year ago. No,

I'm not crazy. I know she's not really there. It's just that some things are too important to let go.

"How do we prepare her for a career? Do we send her to college? Encourage her to join the circus?"

Monica is able to take things in stride in a way that I am not. When I asked her if she'd seen any unusual behavior in Katie, anything remarkable, she said not especially.

"Are you sure?"

"You mean like head spinning, or levitation?" Monica laughed. "No, nothing like that." She wrapped a sweater around her, rainbow knit, navy trim, silver buttons. I didn't recall her having a sweater like that.

I told her about the curtain rod incident I'd walked in on. "Oh, that," she said, smiling. "Enjoy it, Nick. It's a gift."

Sunday morning living room. Cold wind outside, rattling windows. Riffling power lines. Katie on the floor, Play-Doh Fun Factory spread before her. Wavy green strips for grass. Pink and purple trees. I stood on a step stool attaching metal brackets to the window frame with a Phillips screwdriver. Dampness leaked in through cracks in the sill. Across the driveway, our neighbor Lauren, on her porch, rocked her infant son Gregory. In our yard, the plastic climbing structure which, until recently, had been Katie's favorite toy.

"It's not fair," Katie said.

"It's not a tightrope." I turned the screw tight, tested the bracket with my weight. Katie looked up. Looked outside.

"When will Mommy be home?"

Cold wind on my spine. I steadied myself against the wall. "What do you mean?"

She added a midnight blue tree to her landscape. "What time will Mommy be home?"

A restriction in my chest. A flash of anger, followed immediately by the realization that she did not, she could not, mean this to hurt me. I touched her hair. "Mommy's gone, honey. She died. She won't be coming home."

Katie straightened her Play-Doh grass. Wind shook the window. "Oh. Yeah."

A week later, Joel appeared. I hadn't seen my brother-in-law since the funeral, where he seemed to think he alone was entitled to grief. Then, just last month, a dramatic act of extended grieving had landed him in a Montana hospital. He'd called me from there, at two or three in the morning. I'd tried to be sympathetic, but it wasn't my first impulse. Monica had fought so hard to live.

Katie was due home from school any moment. I'd thought it would be her at the door. I'd thought Joel was still in Montana. But there he was, on my doorstep, come to show me his wounds.

He insisted. Right away, first thing when he took off his coat. "Here," he said, rolling up the sleeves of his red flannel shirt. "Look." He turned the cuffs up three folds. I kept an eye on the door, ready to derail Katie. "Look," he commanded, then said, "Here's why you should never, ever use a dull razor." Both our eyes were on the cuts. Inch-long, jagged, scar tissue still tender. Puffy and red. "I'm going to have to develop an interest in cuff links." He waited until our eyes met, held mine for a moment.

I wondered at this gesture. It did keep my eyes from being drawn to his wrists throughout our conversation. Addressed my morbid curiosity and removed one obstacle to us getting on with our friendship.

"What are you going to do?"

"I don't know." Across the street, a group of crows circled the open space where, until last week, an oak tree had stood. Loudly cawed their protest. "I know I don't want to die."

"Good. That's good. "

When Joel was eleven and Monica eighteen, their father had closed himself in the garage one autumn morning, started the car, and drifted off to sleep. Left a note on the dresser that Joel still carries with him. I've never figured out if he believes it will protect him, or if he thinks it will someday explain his own actions. After their father's death, Monica became a second mother, and Joel became melodramatic.

The front door swung open and Katie charged through, backpack trailing behind her. "Daddy!"

She landed in my lap before she saw Joel. Dropped the backpack to the floor. Wrapped her arms around him. Her head on his knee.

"Hey, kiddo," he said, stroking her hair. Joel has his sister's high cheekbones. Her slightly off-balance smile.

She touched the wound on his wrist. "What happened?"

My neck and ears felt hot. Joel beat me to an answer.

"I had an accident."

"Oh. Are you going to die?"

Joel blushed. "I hope not."

"Good." She pulled at his arm. "Wanna play?"

"I have to meet a friend," he said. Katie frowned. Joel was a vapor that appeared and disappeared in our lives. "I wanted to let you know I was in town. This guy's giving me a place to stay."

"Waah. Will you come tomorrow?"

I stood up. "I'm not sure how much Joel will be around, sweetheart."

Katie had moved onto the arm of the chair. Held Joel's sleeve. He met her eyes. "I'll be around as much as you want, kiddo."

You've got to build something from what fragments you can. Leaves. Falling like confetti. Sun not seen in days. Sky the color of a fading bruise. Red maple. Weeping myrtle. The trees Monica taught me to recognize. The cork tree she loved to climb. The smell of the soil in my garden. Walks in the woods. The moments where you plug into your body, where a copper-colored leaf floats by on the wind, bearing snatches of conversation from autumn afternoons. The day Monica told me she was going to have a baby. The day she told me she was going to die. So much goes by unnoticed, it's a victory just to catch a glimpse. To hear a moment pass, to let it carry you. The trick on days like this is to stay warm.

On Sunday afternoons, Katie and I go for ice cream. As much as we can eat. Banana splits. Enormous sundaes. The Trough. We gorge ourselves. Katie can't do quite as much damage as I can. She's five and just a wisp of a thing, but she eats with abandon. It's a ritual we have, and we take rituals seriously.

Two days after Joel's visit, I still walked around in a daze. I couldn't shake the feeling that his arrival made me somehow accountable for his survival and well-being. That he somehow wanted it that way. But he hadn't left any way to reach him, or any clear sense of his destination. Where was he staying? When would I see him? Did I want to?

I had slept late. Left Katie playing in her room while I went downstairs to shower. Came out rubbing my hair dry with a towel. I sensed right away that something was wrong. Shadows. The wrong kind of silence. I reached the base of the stairs and looked up. Perched atop a railing along the second floor hallway, Katie walked, striped in sunlight, arms extended, perfectly poised.

I hurled myself up the stairs, plucked her off the banister, landed her on her bed.

"Dad," she moaned. "What are you doing?"

I shut the door. Paced. Breathed. Fish sheets. Pink comforter. "Do you have any idea how dangerous that is?"

"I was practicing."

"Children play, Katie. Legos are playing. Drawing pictures of ballerinas." I felt dizzy. Rubbed a hand across my face. "How do I get this through to you?" Katie sat on the edge of her bed. Watched me. Frustrated. Curious.

Only one thing occurred to me. I worked hard to keep my voice calm. "You're grounded."

She cocked her head at me. Feet swinging above the floor. Baffled. "What's grounded?"

I sat next to her. Her body so small. Crows complained outside her window. "Tethered," I said. "Safe."

Her eyes on me. Afraid to ask.

I groped for words. "It means you can't do that anymore." I patted her knee. "It means no ice cream today."

Oak leaves dotted the driveway. A gentle wind whirled them around. I watched Katie watch the neighbors out the window. Lauren, on her porch, nursing Gregory in a straight-backed wood chair. Lauren and her partner Sue bought the house a month or two ago. It used to belong to the captain of a merchant ship, an older man, rarely home. Now Lauren does this. Sits quietly. As if she's lurking. But I might be imagining this. After all, it's not my fault Katie's mother died.

Katie's fingers on the window. She had not spoken to me since the grounding. Could not understand. Could not be expected to, as much as I might wish it otherwise. Leaned forward, nose pressed against the glass, face reflected. Her voice, from far away. "Not fair. Gregory has two moms, and I don't have any."

"I need to find a job."

Joel had come by for a visit. Early. Too early. Saturday morning sun poured through living room windows, past the saguaro Monica and I had bought ourselves as a wedding present. Joel sat in an overstuffed chair his mother had given us. I'd made coffee. Katie slept.

"Planning to stay in town?" My stomach muscles tightened. I preferred the idea of supporting Joel via long-distance phone calls.

He nodded. "I think so. I like Boston."

Katie on the phone with him at Christmas. Her birthday. Annual visits. I could be comfortable with that.

"I have you here. Other friends." Joel looked around the room, a room that for him as well as for me must reverberate with hauntings of Monica. An almost imperceptible expectation that she might enter the room at any moment, one you don't even realize you're feeling until you catch yourself marking her absence. "I can learn to be an uncle."

Uncles took children to the park. Pushed them on the swings. Bought them snow cones. Uncles did not slit their wrists.

I sipped coffee. Tucked my feet under me on the couch. Kept quiet.

"It's not that I resented Monica's happiness," Joel said. I stared at the coffee cup he cradled in his hands. At his cuts. A suspicion began to form in the back of my brain: the real reason Joel had come. I couldn't help wondering if Joel's cuts – shorter than I expected, not as deep – represented more a play for attention than a serious attempt on his life. Couldn't help wondering if this were nothing but an elaborate show for our benefit. Katie and I the latest stop on the Joel grief tour. And I hated myself for wondering.

"I envy how easy it seemed for her," he said. "The way she could come home, pop in a movie, eat take-out Chinese from a carton, and be perfectly, unquestioningly content. It's amazing. We grew up in the same house. Ate the same foods."

And unspoken, but understood, *witnessed the same tragedy.*

Joel leaned forward, elbows on knees. Fingers intertwined. "I'm sorry, Nick."

In the end, Monica weak, in constant pain. Joel had promised to come, to help. Decided he couldn't handle it. *I can't see my sister that way.* Warm mug against my fingers. A measure of reassurance. "What do you want me to say? We needed you. It didn't happen. So here we are."

Katie shifted in her bed. Moaned softly.

"I just don't know if I can handle you floating in and out of our lives."

Joel shook his head. "I'm here to stay."

Even he laughed. The spark of humor in his eyes. Joel's face a mirror of Monica. Of Katie. "Maybe it's a chemical imbalance I can correct. Discipline myself into a positive outlook. Prozac my way to happiness."

I'm a wallower myself. But I resented this turning into a sympathy-for-Joel session. The growing feeling that this was all about his need.

Katie wandered in, her eyes half sleepy. Touched my hand. Planted herself in Joel's lap. "What are you talking about?"

Joel balanced her on his knee.

"Grownup stuff," I said. I kissed the top of her head, the part in her fine, sandy hair. Took Joel's empty mug.

In the kitchen, I poured coffee. I didn't want Joel there. Didn't want to help him. To acknowledge our mutual need.

Easy laughter from the living room.

When I returned, sun cast Katie's graceful shadow on the far wall. Atop the couch, she stretched one leg back, into air, reached her arms out, down, to touch the fabric.

Joel applauded. "That's great."

I set down the coffee. My stomach knotted. "Yup. Great. Now get down."

Katie stood on the corner, where the arm meets the back. Balanced. Arms folded. "Da-ad. I'm practicing. Joel's going to teach me a dismount – that's a cool way to get off."

"I know what it is. And he's not teaching you anything. Get down."

Silence hung in the air. Katie obeyed. Stood beside the couch, as if it were a balance beam.

Joel flushed. "What'd I do?"

"Nothing. It's not safe."

"It's fine."

"It's not your decision."

"All I mean is, I used to do it."

I felt myself go cold. "What do you mean?"

"I was a gymnast through high school."

Katie's eyes widened. "Cool!"

I felt as if I were in free fall. No ground in sight.

This memory plays in black-and-white, a vintage film. Ferris wheel at the edge of the Pacific. Santa Monica. Holding hands. Cool breeze blowing grease and salt smells from boardwalk toward ocean, salt and sand from ocean toward boardwalk. Monica and I high above ground, above ocean. Despite my fear. I won't let go, *she said.* Won't let you fall. *The seat we rode in swung back and forth. Squeaks. Suspended in the air, feet dangling, just past the wheel's apex. Nothing under us. Spring sunshine warming our backs. Me squeezing. She:* You're hurting my hand. Relax. *Standing up.* See? It's beautiful. *The wheel jerked down a notch. Monica lurched forward, back. Nearly lost her balance. Laughed. I could see her tumbling into the void. We did not know then that she was dying. Just a Monday afternoon on Santa Monica beach, carousel calliope playing. Monica happy, flying, without a net.*

There's nothing in the book our pediatrician gave us about tightrope walking as a normal developmental phase. I checked. Sat in my den and pored over the text, searching for clues. I was willing to make a reach. It didn't have to specifically mention tightropes. I might have settled for any inclination toward a circus act. But nothing.

"I don't want him around her." I paced in front of the fold-out couch in the den.

Monica hovered in the doorway, arms wrapped around her. "It's getting cold," she said.

"*Monica.*"

"You're overreacting. They share a talent. He wants to help."

I reached for her hand. "You don't think this is scary?"

"I think you're doing great."

"I feel inept."

"She takes after my side of the family."

"That's what I'm afraid of." Nights had begun to turn cold. Frost predicted.

She rubbed my shoulders. "With Dad, it was like he never really belonged to this world." Rested her hands. "Joel is so much like him."

"That's why I don't want him around her."

Monica smiled. "Katie's different. She's like me."

Although Monica's hands felt cold on my shoulders, I didn't want her to move.

"You're telling me you think this is a good idea?"

"She'll be okay. They need each other." Her voice trailed off. She shivered.

"Put a sweater on. You don't want to catch something."

She crossed her arms tight in front of her chest.

"What?" I touched her arm.

She smiled. Her voice low. "I miss her, Nick."

Friday evening. Joel was going to take us to the Children's Museum. I had reluctantly agreed. He was half an hour late.

Katie asked me if I would take down the curtain rod so she could "practice."

"No," I said. "Absolutely not."

She hesitated. Stood with one hand on the couch, her eyes locked on me. "Why?" she said.

"We've talked about this." I tried to remain calm. Patient. "No more. It's not safe."

"I'll put pillows under." She'd pulled her hair into a short ponytail, which made her look older. Like Monica.

"No."

"I can do it," she said, twisting her body in anger. "I need to."

I could feel my teeth grind. "Katie, you're five years old."

"Dad, I already *know* that." Her fingers gripped the upholstery. Dug in. "You never let me do anything."

"The answer is no."

I picked up the phone to call Joel. His roommate answered. Joel wasn't there.

He never showed up. Katie and I ended the evening in her room. She surrounded by stuffed animals. Bears. Kangaroos. Zebra. I tried to explain to her that grownups sometimes forget, and quietly hoped that's all it was.

Katie had the animals divided in two groups.

"What'cha got going there, Katie?"

She pointed. "That's Elizabeth with her four moms, and that's Nina. She's got five moms."

Back yard. Raking leaves. Sun dipping into orange, sinking toward winter. Joel had come to apologize.

"Hey." He stood in the shadow of the myrtle, testing his reception.

I dug into a cluster of leaves, tearing at grass to pull them free. "She was counting on you."

"I couldn't do it." He moved out of the shadow. Hands in pockets. "Where is she?"

A leaf dropped beside me, fiery red, floating. Joel made it so easy to be angry with him, so difficult to express it.

"Grounded."

Joel nodded his head. Smiled a little.

I scooped leaves onto the pan of the rake, held them there with my free hand, tried to deposit them in the bag. Half of them fell to the ground. Joel held the bag open. "Here," he said. "Let me help."

I collected the spillage and tried again.

"You know, I found her walking on the second floor railing. Could have killed herself." I blushed. "Sorry. Figure of speech."

Joel smiled. "Sounds like we've got a situation."

"We?"

"I'd like to help."

I jammed the rake a little too hard into the bag, tearing it a bit.

"It's a little more complicated than missing the Children's Museum," he said. "Some days it just isn't there."

"Fine. Do what you need to do. Get your shit together. Just don't drag Katie down."

"Drag her down?"

Joel held open the thick plastic bag while I scooped in leaves.

"Let's just say you tend to disappear when people are counting on you."

Joel let the bag rest against his leg.

I squinted into sunset to see his face.

"You have no idea how badly I wanted to give myself over to grief."

"Look," Joel said. "I can't promise anything. But I plan to be here." He watched me pick leaves from the metal tines of the rake. "And I'd like to help."

"Yeah? How?" I wanted my voice to sound harsher than it did.

"I have an idea. It would give Katie an outlet, and make it a little safer. More controlled."

Wind stole leaves from the top of the bag. Swirled them at our feet.

"I'm listening."

"We set up a tightrope in the back yard. String something under it as a net."

"No, Joel."

"It's a good idea, Nick. She needs *some*thing."

"Absolutely not."

Steam rose from two mugs, side by side on the coffee table. Earl Grey, honey, lemon. Monica beside me on the couch.

"I can't do it, Monica. There are too many ways she can get hurt. I turn my back for a second. She can burn herself on the stove. Slip in the bathtub. Everyday things. Let alone this." Wind shook the windows. Monica's arm around my shoulder. "I'm so afraid I'm going to lose her."

Monica held me. I wanted to stay there forever.

"You can't keep her from hurt, Nick. As much as you might want to." There were tears in Monica's eyes. Her hands were cold.

I woke with a stiff neck. Street light glowed through the window. It took me a minute to realize I was on the couch. Television on. How many hours had passed? A weather map, garish in orange and magenta. The smell of Earl Grey. Someone in the doorway. I smiled. "Still here?"

"What'cha doing, Dad?" Katie, blanket in hand. Hair tousled. Rubbing her eyes.

My jaw tightened. "Katie, you're supposed to be asleep."

She plopped next to me on the couch. I fought tears. Could feel them escaping down my cheeks.

"What's wrong, Dad?"

A cartoon cloud moved across the weather map, bringing rain to the entire northeast. I put my arm around her, and she nestled into me, her blanket on my chest. I didn't want to be disappointed to see my daughter.

"Nothing, kiddo. I'm just tired."

The blessing and the curse of self-employment is you get to be your own boss. I had become too good at avoiding work. Wednesday afternoon, three-thirty. Katie a few minutes late from school. I stared out the window, which overlooks a hill and a small playground with a spiral slide that Katie has always loved to ride. I pondered what I might cook for dinner.

A shadow caught my attention, out the corner of my eye. I watched. Saw nothing out of the ordinary. Reached for a cookbook. But it happened a second time, my eye drawn to movement outside. This time I let my gaze linger. A cold sensation grew in my belly. I moved to the window.

Katie in air, arms extended, walking slowly, carefully, confidently across the power line that ran between our house and Lauren's.

I've seen squirrels walk that wire. I was not prepared for the sight of my daughter there. It took a minute to register. I opened the window.

"Katie."

She turned her head in surprise, had to steady herself, waving her arms, this five-year-old, twenty feet above solid ground. "Daddy," she said. "What are you doing?"

"What are *you* doing?"

"Practicing."

I breathed deeply. Shifted gears inside. Nodded my head. "Practice is good, honey. Practice is a fine and noble thing. But you're awfully high up."

"I know, Dad, but the important thing is not to look down. Like the Ferris Wheel."

"And that's an electrical wire. It's dangerous. If you touch a part of it that's not covered with rubber, you could be electrocuted." I was trying hard to be the competent parent, responding to a natural phase in my daughter's development.

Katie's voice. "What's electrocuted mean?"

"It means hurt badly. Maybe even killed. Please come back in."

A squirrel hovered on the red maple, on its way toward the wire. Head cocked, it regarded this child in the air, as if trying to connect the moment with the rest of its experience, so that it might know what to do next.

"I just want to cross there." Katie pointed at the corner of Lauren's roof, no more than ten feet beyond her.

"No. Katie. Come back."

A sound drew both Katie's attention and mine. Lauren's head emerged from her second floor window. Her face wore a startled expression. She stared at Katie, at me. I looked back at her.

There seemed little to say. No way to explain.

The squirrel had turned itself sideways on the tree, watching. Wary. Katie's lack of movement was becoming a problem; she teetered.

"Dad, I've got to move." She took a step toward Lauren's house.

I thought about running downstairs with a sheet, following under her, judging wind conditions, gauging the trajectory of a potential fall. But I couldn't make myself move from this place of coaching, coaxing, a place from which I imagined I could take action if needed. I was so close. But a part of me knew the futility. That she was beyond me. That if she truly lost her balance, I was helpless. I couldn't get there in time, even if *I* could walk on air.

Katie wobbled. Took a step for balance. Hovered. Hindered by her concern about disobeying me.

"Dad," Katie said, voice urgent, arms making small circles in the air.

Lauren was less than ten feet away. Eyes alert. Arms ready.

I had no choice. "Do you mind?" I asked her.

Lauren answered without moving her head, without letting her eyes waver from the child who took slow, small steps toward her window. "Not at all." The words, too, came slowly, as if to speak them faster would upset a delicate balance. "That would be fine."

"I'll make hot chocolate," I heard myself say.

I doubt that Lauren even heard me. Her eyes were riveted on Katie's feet, moving a few inches at a time, unerringly toward her goal. We could do nothing but watch as she negotiated the final few steps and sat down on Lauren's window sill, as Lauren wrapped a quick arm around her, and Katie shot me her most triumphant aren't-you-proud-of-me-Daddy smile, before Lauren pulled her inside, and I went downstairs to make hot chocolate.

Some people seem able to hold memories uncomplicated by paradox. Mine are full of contradiction. Fall: a park near Pittsfield. Monica, Katie and I. A family at play. Windex-blue sky. Monica pulling four-month-old

Katie out of the Snuggli, holding her up, in her arms, above her, then down. Mother and daughter, eye to eye, dappled sunlight, spinning slowly, side to side, baby as airplane, the smile up to Katie's eyes. I bent to gather a perfect acorn. Stood to see mother and daughter fall. Disappear from sight. Sound ceased. The universe compressed into the space between my family and myself. Ran, horror images playing in my brain. Looked over a leaf-covered rock ledge. Below, a few feet below, Monica, on her back, in a bed of leaves, Katie held above her, safe, laughing.

Two mugs on the coffee table. Steam rising. Monica gone to get a blanket.

Katie appeared in the doorway. "Can't sleep."

I patted the couch beside me. "Have a seat, kiddo."

She sat. We stared at the glow from the street light. "What'cha thinkin' about, Dad?"

"About your mom."

Katie touched my knee, traced a line with her index finger. "What was she like?"

Pain fresh, a wound re-opened moment by moment. "What do you remember?" I could hear Monica puttering through the linen closet.

"She had a pretty voice. She used to sing me the song without words."

Echoes of a voice. A melody.

October afternoon. Liver-colored sky. Yellowing leaves dotted the back yard maple. Returning from a meeting on the North Shore, I parked the car, gravel crunching under tires. Heard Katie, her laugh, in the back yard, Joel encouraging her.

I walked back. "Hey."

Katie, perched on a rope Joel and I had strung from myrtle to maple in our back yard, three hammocks bridging the gap underneath, providing the security I needed.

"Hi, Daddy." Katie walking toward me on the rope, gracefully, naturally. I had to remind myself she wasn't on the ground. Joel, the proud coach, watching.

I touched Joel's elbow. He grinned. On the porch next door, Gregory dozed in Lauren's arms, tucked close to her chest. "Katie's been practicing something for you," Joel said. "She hasn't quite got it, but she's close."

A scattering of fallen leaves had begun to cover the climbing structure, the domain of other children her age.

"Do I want to see this?"

Lauren's voice wafted across the driveway, a distant lullaby.

"What do you think, Katie? Are you ready to show your Dad?"

"Sure."

Joel looked over at me. A yellow leaf drifted past his ear. "Brace yourself," he said.

I sat on the grass, legs crossed.

Katie turned, her back to me. Took three steps away and hurled herself backward, into air, into sky, legs gently propelling, upside down, floating above the rope, my body resisting the urge to leap forward, to catch her, her feet spinning back toward earth. Out of the corner of my eye I could see Joel, smiling, confident. Katie's face a big, blurry grin. In her element. *Where did this come from? Where will it lead?* I can't answer those questions. What I can do is wait for Katie to land, and hold her while she's here.

Las Vegas Wedding
Or, Buffy the Vampire Slayer Meets Gertrude Stein at the Luxor

THE WEDDING WAS TO BEGIN at 11 am.

There was no talk of time zones, of Eastern Standard versus Mountain versus Pacific (viewers on the West Coast will see the wedding at its regularly scheduled time), of the orientation required after a long plane flight.

There were people coming in from Minnesota (Gertrude, as it turns out), North Carolina, Massachusetts, and California. There was one on her way from Russia, and several who wished to breakfast in Paris. There were foot-long hot dogs for 99 cents, announced like movies on giant marquees. There were margaritas available by the yard. There were no clocks, anywhere.

I'm not making excuses. I'm just saying that under these conditions, orientation is not as easy as you might think. The compass insisted that West was down. That North was up.

1.
Gertrude said, "People if you like to believe it can be made by their names. Call anybody Paul and they get to be a Paul."

Ω

Call me Paul. Call her Christine. Place us on a corridor, leaning against a railing and looking down at the Attractions Level of the Luxor Hotel in uncertain light. Two stories below, under glass, couples ambled arm in arm. A line formed outside the Imax theater. We'd sought momentary refuge. Fresh air.

The Luxor Hotel is a glass pyramid with more than 4,400 rooms. It is one of eight objects on earth that is identifiable when seen from the space shuttle. It is a confusing place, even if you haven't just missed your brother's wedding.

Sometimes you can see your way to the top, a reverse stairstep effect where the sides climb to an eventual convergence. But things cut in at strange angles everywhere. Corridors. Inclinators. Tiny hallways that end in doors marked Staff Only. Sometimes there is a ceiling just inches above your head.

"Feels nice to be outside," Christine said.

I nodded agreement. It was as if we could feel a light wind stir around us, as if we could anticipate a sunset. But when our eyes sought horizon, they found borders. Walls where sky should be. The Attractions Level a false city below us, a world within a world.

"How do you get down there," she said, disheartened.

The hotel brochure suggested that guests may want to bring a small pocket compass. We did. We are not people who take orientation for granted.

I took the compass from my pocket. She looked to me for direction, because it wasn't my brother whose wedding we couldn't find.

"It says West is that way," I said, pointing down.

Δ

For access to the Attractions Level, use central elevators located inside the casino.

again.

The wedding was to begin at 11am.

We were to meet in the lobby at 10:30, which does not leave much margin for error; for confusion or disorientation; for those who somehow do not set their watches to local time and have repeatedly to do the math; or for Chip the Surfer from San Diego (he was Best Man) to get his picture taken with the woman the hotel employs to stand at the casino entrance in a toga and share her breasts with all who walk by.

Chip insisted on a Polaroid.

It was 10:40. We had to find the others and drive to the Candle-light Chapel of Love. Only the groom knew where it was.

Ω

The thing about a pyramid is that it's difficult to orient yourself inside. Sometimes you find yourself looking up at Ramses, other times you're in the presence of the man with the ferret head as he bets a hundred dollars on red. And you haven't even been drinking yet.

again.

We descended in parallel elevators.

It seemed incredible that we could lose one another. We met up at 10:30, emerged from our rooms and walked down the hall, the whole wedding party in one place.

Christine and I rode with Chip the surfer, and Christine's parents. We pressed L for Lobby. I can't say what they pressed.

We got off, and they weren't there. We figured they had stopped somewhere, maybe the Attractions Level. Then we thought maybe they'd landed before us. We went looking for the lobby.

On our way, we passed the casino entrance, where Chip had his picture taken with the woman with the amazing breasts. There's no chance her breasts were real. But that's the thing about Las Vegas. As long as you accept it, it can be quite beautiful.

The desert air. The swimming pools.

They weren't in the lobby, either. We looked all over. Went outside to where the valets were. Nothing. 10:45. Chip decided he'd go looking. Maybe they went to get the limo and would meet us out front. Maybe they were having their picture taken with the woman with the amazing breasts. Maybe, inspired by her example, they were having their own breasts enhanced.

2.

Gertrude said, "There is no use telling more than you know, even if you do not know it."

Ω

In Episode 57, just before the carnage begins, before Buffy engages in a few rounds of kick-boxing with Spike and wrests from him the all-powerful Gem of Ankarra, Buffy and Willow have a moment to just be freshmen, for Buffy to tell Willow about her date. Her new boyfriend. For Buffy to glow. Then Willow says: "I love this part. Don't you love this part, where everything's new and mysterious."

again.

I wasn't worried.

It wasn't my Las Vegas wedding. There was nothing we could do but shrug and give ourselves to the moment.

Christine's father turned to me and said, "We're going to miss the wedding."

That was when time became fuzzy. The Candlelight Chapel of Love books weddings every 15 minutes.

Christine's parents went to play the quarter slots. "We'll be right there," her father said, pointing to a row of machines we would never see again.

Δ

For feelings of abandonment, or issues surrounding the absence of a loved one, use Inclinator #3.

again.

We liked Ramon best. We trusted Ramon.

We liked saying "Put it all on odd." We began drinking vodka tonics. The waitress brought them. We had a stack of lime green chips, and the desire to spend big. We always kept something on number three.

The casino had a burgundy carpet. Ornate wallpaper. Ramon wore a brocade vest, a white shirt. We believed in Ramon.

There were always the same players at Ramon's table. Gertrude. Christine and I. The man with the ferret head. Skinny body, long neck, a maple leaf lapel pin, a head that swerved and leaned slowly and at odd angles. He kept ogling Christine. He had the best view of the wheel. Even so, he would lean in as the ball landed, swivel down and around so that he was at eye level with the wheel, his head flopped to the side.

Christine grabbed a fresh drink from the waitress' tray. "What time is it?" she asked. Without looking, the waitress replied, "Quarter to nine." We believed her.

The number three came up a lot.

Gertrude, all wrinkles and concentration and chain-smoking bemusement. Her hair was shorter than in the pictures I'd seen. She wore jeans, and a thick leather belt with one of those giant belt buckles, a coiled snake.

We put a hundred dollars on twenty-three. Twenty on three. Nothing was real.

"People if you like to believe it can be made by their names," Gertrude said. A halo of cigarette smoke surrounded her. It was not clear to whom she was speaking. "Call anybody Paul and they get to be a Paul." The white ball spun around the wheel. We put a hundred dollars on seventeen, forty on three. "What's your name?" Her eyes found mine.

"Paul," I said.

She nodded. Smiled. Smoked.

Ω

Elvis Costello on the Attractions Level. Two shows nightly.

and then:

There were times we needed rest. We spent an afternoon by the pool. Watched the sunset. We had regular sessions with Ramon. Gertrude. The man with the ferret head. Wads of bills made their way into our pockets.

Once, we found the room. The pocket compass was no help.

There was a fake lotus plant in one corner. There were champagne and real fruit, compliments of the hotel. Christine had used the Luxor to entice me. Mostly, though, the need was real.

"Please come," she'd said. "I'm not sure I can get through this wedding alone."

I was happy to go. Las Vegas and all.

"What did I miss?" She emerged from the bathroom, traces of toothpaste at the side of her mouth.

I lay propped in bed, remote in hand, pillows stacked behind me. Buffy on the tube. "Spike found the gem and he's now invincible as long as he's wearing it – you can stab him with a stake and it heals right up."

Ω

Episode 62
Buffy's Las Vegas Wedding

In which Buffy interrupts the nuptials of her alleged foster brother just in time when Jean-Claude, the French-Canadian minister at the Candlelight Chapel of Love, pins a boutonniere on the best man, and draws blood. The sight of his best man's blood causes a glow in her faux brother's eyes that sets off Buffy's sixth sense. She stops the show in grand fashion, halting the wedding, and punching the big guy's ticket for good. "I should have known something was wrong," Buffy later confides to Willow. "Foot-long hot dogs? How Wayne Newton."

and then:

The man with the ferret head leaned in for a closer look.

The felt was bright green. We liked the sheen of it. We felt lucky. Felt odd. Christine had managed, for the moment, to forget about the wedding. She held a vodka tonic and a wad of bills.

"Always," Christine said. "Always bet on odd."

The ball stopped on seventeen. Gertrude watched Ramon sweep away a stack of her lavender chips.

"I have had a long and complicated life," said Gertrude. She placed a stack of chips on a rectangle marked 1-12. "I am very busy finding out what people mean by what they say," she said. "Say this: There is no use telling more than you know, no not even if you do not know it."

I said it. Gertrude nodded. She liked me. The ball stopped on three.

You could bet individual numbers. You could bet red or black, odd or even. You could bracket numbers. We believed in odd. The man with the ferret head kept ogling Christine.

But then she spotted him. Chip. Across the casino. The mustache. The ineffable grin. We left two sizable stacks of lime green chips on the table and took off after him.

3.
Buffy: "That's beautiful or, taken literally, incredibly gross."
Gertrude: "Time is not one thing following another."

and then:

We followed Chip and Gertrude followed us and somehow we found ourselves on the Attractions Level, with no Chips. Gertrude had cashed us out and handed us a wad of bills. It was well over two thousand dollars.

"Time is being alive really alive in the moment, right now and right now and right now."

"Excuse me." Christine stopped a woman walking past an exhibit called In Search of the Obelisk, "Do you know what time it is?"

We were on the Attractions Level, contained in a magnificent pyramid. We were visible from space.

Christine held the woman's arm. The woman held a large vinyl purse and a cell phone. She consulted her wrist watch without moving her head. "Quarter to nine," she said, and then she was gone.

Gertrude had a cigarette burning in each hand. "Right now and right now and right now," she said.

Christine held the wad of bills in her left hand. "Fuck and fuck and fuck and fuck," she said.

I worried that she and Gertrude were edging toward a stripped-down syntax I would not comprehend. I soothed myself with thoughts of Bavarian creme doughnuts and coffee with real half-and-half.

Christine's gaze had developed an intensity. Half a floor below us, we could see the lobby, a 30-foot-tall Nefertiti and Ramses, a diminutive Sphinx. She searched the crowd.

She slapped my arm with the wad of bills. Pointed with her free hand. "There!" In the lobby. In motion. Chip. She tossed the bills in our general direction, hurdled the rail. I swear she floated toward the lobby floor.

There was nothing to do but follow.

Ω

Episode 73 (revised)
Buffy Meets Gertrude Stein at the Luxor Las Vegas

When the body count begins to pile up at the resort hotel's pool, Buffy and the great modernist literary figure team up to take down a nocturnal aqua killer. "What is a vampire," Gertrude says in the pivotal third act, "and if you know what is a vampire then what is Las Vegas."

what came next:

It all happened fast. There was a white mini-van parked at the entrance to the hotel. There was no longer a watch, but Chip was convinced we had time.

Yes. We found Chip. He refused to get his picture taken with Gertrude, who had twisted her ankle in the leap to the lobby.

"There is a difference," she said, "between what I like and what they like." A tiny stub of cigarette burned from her lip. I hadn't yet told her she was a hero to me. "Welling is changed from William to welcome. In willing."

I stayed between she and Christine. I was afraid Christine might be unwilling. I dreamed of doughnuts.

Chip stared blankly at Gertrude.

I could see the van outside, beyond two sets of automatic doors.

As we emerged, I could also see something else: Buffy and Willow, striding toward us. We nearly knocked them over.

They were filming episode 73, in which they expose and then bludgeon a roulette dealer/vampire who had been living in a crypt in the lobby of the Luxor Las Vegas. At this point in Act 3, Buffy and Willow were supposed to enter the hotel lobby cocky-scared, in that way they do. Cameraman poised before them, his back to the door, bent in a determined half-squat, standing on a wooden cart with a metal handle on one end, which a production assistant wheeled toward the entrance.

Through the glass doors they could see Ramses and Nefertiti, in stone three stories tall.

"Freaksome," said Buffy.

"Power-freaksome," said Willow.

The camera tracked their movement. The cameraman wore a green baseball cap. Chip was transfixed.

Christine apoplectic. "I am quite sure we do not have time for this." A cloud of cigarette smoke followed us.

We could see the van, behind Buffy and Willow.

Gertrude hacked up phlegm.

The only way we were going to get Chip into the vehicle was to get a Polaroid.

4.

Gertrude said, "Whenever they are liable to have an emergency they are just as likely to do it slowly."

and then:

We were in a white mini-van, careening north on The Strip. Christine, myself and Chip, Buffy and Willow and Gertrude. Gertrude drove, erratic, cursing, following the limo we believed contained the bride and groom.

"Fuck and fuck and fuck and fuck and fuck," she said. One cigarette dangled from her lips. Another burned in each hand. "I am very busy finding out how to stay with this limo."

She swerved. She weaved. She coughed. She dodged traffic. The van listed, felt as if it would tip.

Gertrude, it turned out, was a Buffy fan. "Among the clothes that just don't look like Buffy are button-front shirts and anything in the color red," she said. She swerved around a black pickup, kept the limo in sight. She was a repository of Buffy trivia. "Total number of Buffy outfits the first three seasons: three hundred twelve."

Willow had placed herself between Chip and Buffy. Had cracked open the back windows. Even so, a haze of smoke lingered. We passed a hotel called Paris.

"The last time I was here, Paris wasn't open yet," Chip said. "They hadn't finished the Eiffel Tower."

Gertrude swerved left. Chip's head bounced against the window. "First time Buffy admits to her Dorothy Hamill obsession," Gertrude said. "Episode twenty-one."

Christine had filled Buffy in on the way. The wedding. The cast of characters.

Buffy was game. "Time to kick some demon ass," she said. Chip stared at her breasts.

Δ

For access to an alternate reality featuring nubile television performers, use Inclinator #2.

and then:

We found the chapel. Screeched in a minute or so behind the limo, cutting off a Hilton courtesy van to make the last turn. No one was seriously hurt. It was right next to Circus Circus. And a food stand with a giant marquee, foot-long hot dogs and Fresca, 99 cents each. We were early.

No one seemed surprised to see us, or aware that anything unusual had transpired. Or surprised that we had with us a literary figure from a previous century and two young television stars. We acted casual. We didn't want to be out of step with local culture.

"Psst," Christine's father said. He was eating a peppermint stick ice cream cone. He motioned to us with his head, the way people do. Christine hugged him. It was the hug of someone who had given up the idea of ever seeing her father again, but not overtly.

The bride and groom sat in a white latticed gazebo, surrounded by roses, having their photographs taken. The foot-long hot dog marquee in the background. I made a mental note to get copies of the wedding pictures.

"Look," Christine's father said. He was an Albanian man wearing a black leisure suit with huge pockets. He held one open and encouraged us to look inside. It was filled with quarters. So was the other one.

Christine's stepmother, who spoke very little English, held up her purse with both hands and shook it. It too was filled with coins.

"We hit the jackpot," Christine's father said.

The wedding went off without a hitch. As much an event as you can have in fifteen minutes. Bride. Groom. Parents. Sister. Sister's strange friend. Buffy. Willow. Gertrude, who kept at least two cigarettes going at all times and continuously snapped pictures with her cell phone. And the man with the ferret head, who of course turned out to be Jean-Claude, the French-Canadian minister.

He did a nice job. He told them they could have every expectation of happiness.

30

Gertrude waited patiently to congratulate the happy couple, who greeted her as if she were family, even though she dropped ash on the groom's pants. "They are washable," she said. "They are found and able and edible."

Buffy and Willow also paid their respects. "I'm sensing major sparkage," said Buffy. "Serious wow potential, " Willow echoed.

Chip huddled by the chapel entrance in intense conversation with Jean-Claude. At his side, the woman with the amazing breasts. I didn't even *want* to know how that happened.

Christine and I stood arm in arm.

Sunshine beamed down. I couldn't tell if we were really outdoors. I didn't care.

"Well," she said. "We did it."

Through the latticework I could see the giant marquee: 99 cents. I felt in my pocket, fingered the wad of bills. I felt magnanimous. "Come on," I told Christine. I took out the pocket compass and headed for the hot dog stand.

South of Why

IT'S THREE A.M. ON A TUESDAY and Frank's got his head in my toilet.

He says he's in love with a woman he's never met. We've been drinking and arguing about it since dinner. Not the morality of it. I'm not entitled to the moral high ground in matters of relationship. We've argued the logistics. The conceptual possibilities. I've argued, strenuously and to no avail through a barbecue dinner and several vodka tonics, that it's impossible to be in love with someone you've never seen.

Right now Frank's making horrible noises in the bathroom and I'm holding the cordless phone to my ear, listening to Frank's wife Julie and thinking about what I'm going to say when she stops talking.

Julie is mad at me. Wants me to tell Frank to go home. But even if I think he's acting like an idiot, which I do, he's been my friend forever. Julie isn't going to grasp the significance of that at the moment. She holds me somehow responsible for Frank's would-be romance, though in recent months I've spent more time with her than with him. She's shouting into the phone about emotional infidelity. *On-line intercourse*, she says. *Adultery*. When I question her about it – you don't mean that? – she accuses me of having a faulty moral structure. *Relativist*, she says. *Godless prick*.

Yes, I tell her – I'm interrupting but I can't help it, my head is starting to hurt – my sense of a moral system *has* collapsed and your husband *does* claim to be in love with a woman he's never met, but that doesn't make you right.

Julie launches into further invective, so that I have to hold the phone away from my ear to keep it from hurting. I can still hear her clearly at arm's length. *Sex for cowards,* she says. *Computer as condom.*

My wife Anna is asleep on the couch. Anna has no patience for this. After all, it's three a.m. on a Tuesday and she doesn't approve of me hanging out with religious fanatics. Anna distrusts extremism of any kind. Even excessive devotion to one person. That's why she sleeps around periodically, to protect herself from getting hurt. Me, I'm intrigued by faith. It isn't as easy as people think. I know I'm not up to the work. For instance, here's Julie reading me Bible verses over the phone. Still shouting. *Love,* she says, *is patient. Love is kind. Is not envious.*

I know what I need to do here. Keep Julie going until there's a moment of silence in the bathroom. So I can bring the phone and Frank can say a few words that will halt the slide toward separation.

From where I stand in the hallway of the Boston Victorian that Anna and I have somehow refurbished in our thirteen years of on-again, off-again cohabitation, I can see Frank's body hunched over the toilet and hear his grunts, his groans that sound like he's enduring personal Armageddon. My Irish setter Dante stands watch, just inside the doorway, perfectly still. Perplexed. Intent. He's not leaving there until he understands this. I can see Anna's sweet body sprawled on the couch, book still in hand.

The couch, by the way, is amazing. People always remark on how comfortable it is. We had it built. It's jade green and puffy, and you can't possibly stay awake if you lay down on it. Julie has lusted after it for years. One night Frank, drunk and invincible, tried to hoist it on his back and steal it for her.

For now we see in a mirror, dimly, Julie is saying, one of my favorite Bible verses, and I say the rest of it along with her which she doesn't appreciate because tonight, she wants, and probably deserves, the moral high ground, *but then we shall see face to face.* I can't help smiling at the irony. Because Frank, you know, hasn't.

Anna hates the desert. Despises it. Anna had a bad relationship, in her early twenties, in a small town in Arizona. Bisbee. Lived with this guy for two years. I can't remember his name and she won't speak it, but he had an interesting house. Filled with artifacts from copper mines. Anyway, this guy was incredibly possessive, and she put up with it until the day he locked her in the house and took her keys because she'd had lunch with another guy. She says it wasn't until she was locked in that she realized she could leave. And she did. Out a window. Left the man. Left Bisbee. Left Arizona. Never been back.

She has nothing good to say about the desert.

There are two versions of Frank's story. Both more or less true.
A.

Frank sits in his office late one night, scanning the electronic bulletin board for something to divert him. He's been working too many late hours for too long, developing computer systems for companies around the world. Maybe he's listening to Counting Crows, or maybe to a Mahler symphony, and he wanders into a room he's never visited before. A trivia game and conversation room. There's a note there, posted for everyone. A woman asking for information about an occasional visitor – Melvin.

"This Melvin has been harassing her," Frank tells me, sitting in Redbones, polka band playing in the background. "Private messages. Explicit. This happens from time to time. Morons with no life. Usually, you confront them, they disappear. She asks the guy to leave her alone. To stop sending messages. But he won't." We're into our third

round of drinks, and the food hasn't arrived yet. "She changes her
e-mail address, and he still finds her."

"She says all this in the note?"

"Course not," he says. Plates appear before us – pulled pork,
brisket. "Most of this I find out later. Anyway, she contacts the online
police, they boot the guy off the service. Problem solved, or so she
thinks."

"Online police?" I'm waving an empty vodka glass hoping to get
the waiter's attention. The place is packed.

Frank explains to me about the officers who patrol the electronic
highway. "They investigate complaints about harassment. Misuse of
the system. They can remove people if there are repeated complaints."

I envision computer-generated cartoon officers wandering the
on- and off-ramps of the electronic highway, twirling their cartoon
billy clubs and doffing their hats to familiar faces. "Amazing," I say. I
picture Frank in his office, typing away, conversing with the cartoon
police officer on his screen. A chubby man in a tight blue coat with a
bulldog face and an oversized silver badge pinned to his chest. Frank
pushing an arrow key every now and then to make the cartoon officer
jump in place.

The polka band launches into something I remember from
watching Lawrence Welk with my grandmother as a child. Frank and
I need to do this more often. Hanging out. Making sense of things.
Frank explains to me how he sat in his office, staring out the window,
through the reflection of his fluorescent lights and his protracted self,
thinking about this woman. "The guy was back in less than a week.
Under another name. Finds her again. She has no idea how."

Even now, talking about what happened, Frank's face flushes
with anger. He's trying to tell me how it was. He's trying to tell me
he's lonely. I want to tell him I understand, but I've never been good
at the code of the half-spoken.

What happened that night in his office: Frank gets angry. Frank
stares at his pale reflection in the window. Frank sends a message to

this woman, identifying with her isolation. He sends it anonymously, expects and wants no reply. "It's a way to vent, you know? To let her know that not everyone out there is an asshole."

But she writes back.

Anna grew up near Bisbee. The closest town was a place called Why. Anna grew up south of there, an area that had no name, just dust and dirt and scrub and ocotillo, and this little brown house her father had built in the middle of it all.

Anna's father worked in the National Park Service, a ranger at the Organ Pipe Cactus National Monument. He filled his house with books and taught his children about nature and traveled with them on vacations so they would have an awareness of other places. But he didn't know much about people, and Anna's mother left when Anna was six, because she couldn't handle the loneliness. And there's a hard place in Anna now, which time and I wear away at, but only slowly. It was marked there, in that house, in that desert, and hard as I've tried, I can't understand that kind of distance.

When Anna moved after high school, it was to Bisbee, about a hundred and fifty miles from Why along two-lane desert highways. Bisbee: every third building a forgotten miner's tavern. Bisbee: the vitality clawed out of the earth, leaving vast, rust-colored craters. As years pass, the sun bakes the color even out of those, leaving them dishwater gray. Only in the mountains above the city do you find the tentative green of juniper leaves and the occasional yellow blossom of a prickly pear. Anna's move from nowhere to a dead city was her way, she says, of easing herself into the world.

When she first told me all this, when we met, I said come on. It sounded too much like some television movie about a woman fighting for custody of her child. Anna just looked at me, not knowing how to respond.

Anna turns over on the couch, burrows into a near-fetal position, merges herself into the back cushions, while from the sounds of the ordeal in the bathroom Frank is in danger of flushing his upper intestine. Dante maintains his strange vigil: quiet, intent, head leaning in to get a better view, body holding back, cautious. Only the back of Frank's head is visible, shaking in spasms above the toilet bowl. I want to slap him, to warn him not to wake up Anna, but I'm afraid to go in there. I don't want Julie to hear his convulsions through the receiver. Somehow, she's into the parables. *The earth produces of itself, first the blade, then the ear, then the full grain in the ear.* I don't know how we got here. I confess I'm not fully listening. *He who has ears to hear, let him hear.*

Despite this, I like Julie. Her fire. The way she goes from holy to vulgar in a microsecond. It's sexy. Besides, you've got to realize they've been fighting hard for three days, and she hasn't slept much.

Here's how they fight: Julie yells and Frank throws things. Then Julie calls me, and we have these talks. One time I was at their house after a major blow-up, and I followed the trail of yolk stains to find them. Frank likes to throw eggs. Don't ask me why.

I have a 1981 Rand McNally Road Atlas that has seen me across the country three times, and accompanied me on countless shorter trips. Each major trip I've made, I've highlighted on the map the route I took, noted dates and traveling companions where applicable. I love to take out that atlas – it's barely hanging together now, love and packing tape – and look through it, sometimes even trace the lines with my fingers. Purple lines, mostly older, that trace my travels with Frank. Blue lines to document my journeys with Anna. Scattered reds, greens and yellows track adventures with college friends or old lovers. Stretches of road are alive in my mind. And places, like this diner in Pennsylvania, where I had an early morning breakfast with Frank, who was living in Cleveland at the time. Or the National Peanut Monument in Blakely, Georgia which Anna and I drove two hundred miles out of our way to see, expecting I suppose something grandiose, some majestic tribute to the labors of the American farmer, but found (and it was difficult to find) instead a two-and-a-half foot high slab of concrete, like a tombstone, with a carved peanut on the top that you would only recognize if you had driven two hundred miles out of your way to see it. But we had time, Anna and I, and we took pictures of each other standing next to it, and we laughed ourselves all the way to Atlanta. You can't say that wasn't worth it.

Frank moved a lot in the years right after college. Had a fear of going someplace he'd already lived. Saw it as failure. I stayed in Boston. We'd meet in strange places, halfway points, for breakfast, or a late-night drink. Then drive all the way back. It was a concrete form of support. A promise of commitment. I don't know when Frank's wanderlust changed, or if. I suspect it didn't and that's why he wanders the electronic highways. Me, I go for long drives. Once I found myself in Chicago. Drove through the night and into the next day, stopping only for gas and bathrooms. Like Frank, I'm afraid to stop. Afraid to inhabit the silence that would result.

Then I remember the phone in my hand. "That's right," I say to Julie. "The chaff from the wheat."

There's a pause on the line. So I jump in. I want to make some inroads here. Pave the way for reconciliation until Frank can make his way to the phone. I'm hopeful. The bathroom is quieter. I say to Julie, I can understand that you're hurt. I want to show her how it's not such a big deal. Really, I say to her. I know it's hard, but put it in perspective. I don't know any guy who hasn't been emotionally unfaithful, *at least* once.

Well this was the wrong thing to say because her voice, which had started to settle down, is back at fever pitch and she's asking me *has this happened with Frank before?* Even if it had I couldn't possibly tell her, because Frank and I have a sacred trust. So I'm kicking myself for setting her off again and wishing I could wake up Anna, but she'd kill me. By the way, Anna tells me later that she agrees with Julie on this, one hundred percent. That there's nothing worse than a man taking his emotional intimacy to another woman. And I'm surprised to hear Anna agree with Julie on anything, but then I think I should have learned this about her by now. And if I can, it will increase the possibility of Anna and I lasting another thirteen years.

The first time Anna and I split up, it was over Why. I planned a trip there with Frank. I'm crazy about her. I wanted to see where she came from. Wanted to walk the ground she had walked. See if it would help me understand the desert part of her. But she didn't like the idea. She saw it as betrayal. An attempt to extract from her something vital. I don't know why I went after that, but the angrier she got, the more desperate I was to see it.

So we went, Frank and I. Even stayed a few days in Bisbee. It's actually a great town. I've been several times since. Frank smoothed things out with Anna after that first trip. Explained to her that it was a pilgrimage, a journey of love, a testimony of devotion. As moving as his speech was, though, that's not what convinced her to forgive. It was when she realized that, despite my efforts, I wasn't able to pry loose any insight from the land.

Anna and I have never been deeply shaken by each other's infidelities. It's the little stuff that's nearly done us in. Like the time I acted as counselor – consoler – for Diane, who was going through a painful divorce. A phone call, late into the night, when Anna wanted to talk, and fell asleep waiting for me. When I woke in the morning, she was gone. That one took a year to put back together. Of course, it was more than one phone call. But still, people have such different ideas of what's forgivable.

Uh-oh. Something has upset the delicate balance in the bathroom. Frank is sounding like a malfunctioning septic system. Dante growls tentatively from the bathroom doorway. This can't be a good thing. Dante tends to be skittish, and Irish setters aren't the brightest dogs. We had hopes of educating him but he's ten years old and hasn't learned much. I try to imagine the look on his face right now. He's not used to seeing humans with their heads in the toilet. Thank God Frank can't see him. Who knows what would happen.

Julie wants to know why. Why he's going somewhere else. And among the many answers I could give her that range the full spectrum from her side to his, I settle on one: That's not for me to say.

Well how would you feel, she asks, and I'd love to answer her, but I want to move this along, and you have to go so slowly with people. Like me. It's taken me years to see something Anna has tried patiently to teach me. You can't extract trust. Even the people you're closest to have hidden places, and you can't tear into that confidence. That has to be given, and held so, so gently, to keep it from breaking.

B.

In the second version of Frank's story, it's all about banter.

I'm comfortable, walking a slow circle in my dining room, my best friend retching in my toilet, my faithful dog keeping watch, my wife asleep on the couch. It's beginning to feel homey.

Think about it, Julie says. *It's got all the qualities of an affair. Late-night talks. Secret meetings.* She says: *What do you call it when a person stays up all night being intimate with someone?*

There are all kinds of intimacy, I'm thinking. Theirs, at least at first, was the intimacy of banter. Lists of ten worst movies ever (excluding karate flicks). Vacation spots you'd never want to visit. Sounds harmless, I say, but Julie cuts in. *I don't think they stayed up all night talking about bad movies.* I happen to know she's right about that one. But the banter gave Frank a way to open up. A place to begin talking. Julie's not finished. *Besides,* she says, *banter is simply a substitute for oral sex.*

She's saying this just to piss me off. Banter is a sacred tradition among men, I say.

It's a power thing – another way for men to be on top.

BULLSHIT! It's an underappreciated art. Men dream of a woman who can hold her own with banter. Just like we dream of a woman who can do the Three Stooges finger-snapping thing.

Great, Julie says. *I want a relationship and he wants snappy dialogue and snapping fingers.*

I consider complimenting her on her banter, but think better of it. Instead I tell her I've got a friend who has remained romantically unattached for years because he has yet to meet a woman he could banter with. I'm the wrong person for her to talk to about this. I understand loneliness, and tend to feel that whatever soothes it is okay. Whatever gets you through.

Why? Julie asks, and I want to say to her, but I don't: why makes me nervous. Because there isn't always a reason for things, or a way of explaining that renders them sensible. I'm trying hard to accept what is and work with that.

Women want intimacy, she says. *Men want sex.*

This is ground I'm willing to defend. Not true, I insist. I'm apoplectic. I want to call Frank out here to defend himself, to defend the sacred traditions of men, the means – however imperfect – that we find to unveil ourselves. But he's preoccupied. "How can you say that? She and Frank have never even met."

Electronic insertion, she says. *Mental masturbation. The on-line affair is a chickenshit way out of a real one. Men think it's safe sex because they don't have to get involved, or deal with the emotional consequences. I'm tempted to buy him a plane ticket. Let them do a soul roll so we can get on with our lives.*

I tell her I'm shocked to hear a religious person talking this way.

Fuck you, she says. It's three a.m. She's pulling out all the stops. *Be his friend. Tell him to come home.*

I've got a problem with the idea of monogamy. So does Anna. Though she'd never admit it, we've both proven it by our actions. Seems to me it just creates problems, this expectation of fidelity. This definition of faithfulness. Or maybe we're just a generation so accustomed to betrayal we've come to expect it, to be in fact more comfortable with it. I guess we all have our sensitive areas, though. Like this: Anna likes to hear my secrets. The only thing that makes her jealous is if I take my secrets somewhere else, or another woman takes hers to me. And me: the thought of Anna sleeping on someone else's couch. Of her being comfortable enough to do that. I'd rather she lay pipe with someone I don't like.

Frank has begun moaning my name, softly, in the bathroom. At first, I think this is a good sign. I even allow myself a little smile. I'm ready to bring him the phone. But then Dante, still poised in the doorway, sits on his haunches and howls, like he does when he hears a siren.

Julie wants to know what's going on. *I want answers,* she says.

This isn't a good time to explain, I tell her. I'm afraid that Anna's going to wake up and be pissed that I'm getting involved in this. I'm looking for something to throw at Dante, but it's too late. Frank looks up from the toilet bowl, from his stupor. I can see his humbled self through the doorway.

Something – the expression on Frank's face or maybe just the gray-green color of it, sends Dante running, with two sharp barks, into the living room. To his credit, he tries to stop (he has learned *something* these ten years), but the wood floors are newly refinished. I can see it coming but I can't stop it.

Dante sliding across the living room floor, limbs akimbo, scratching his paws fruitlessly on the polished wood, turning his head around to look at me, to plead with me, to let me know that he is, he really is, trying to stop.

Movement in the bathroom, and, though I'm transfixed by my dog's balletic slow motion slide, in my peripheral vision I swear I see Frank standing up, and I say to Julie, This is beautiful, even though I know she won't understand, and that it's going to get ugly any second now – Frank should NOT be walking.

I'm so proud of Dante – his efforts to stop himself, his awareness that all hell is about to break loose – that I don't make a move to stop anything. I just brace for the crash, and say to Julie, you'll have to hold on and then – contact – Dante hits, the full force of his sixty pounds crashes into the table behind the sofa.

The table teeters. The ceramic lamp hovers in mid-air. Julie says into the phone, *WHAT DO YOU MEAN HOLD ON?* I definitely hear footsteps moving slowly, so slowly, from the bathroom. Dante tries to regain control of his body, to move his dog bulk out of the trajectory of falling objects. The table is going down. The only question is whether it will fall on the lamp or the lamp on it. I can't help marveling at the slow-motion quality of it all. It's poetry. Pure Sam Peckinpah.

Boom. Shards of pottery and light-bulb glass squirt everywhere, skitter across the floor.

Dante howls. The table has caught him on a hind leg.

Julie's voice: *What's happening? Are you there?*

Nearly lost in all this is Frank's emergence from the bathroom, white towel around his neck, eyes puffy, drops of liquid clinging to his chin. He looks like someone recently exhumed.

Julie's voice demands to know what happened.

I don't say anything, as if my silence will preserve some sense of calm. But I know what's going to happen, and it does. Anna's head emerges, slowly, inexorably, above the back of the sofa. The first thing visible is the part in the middle of her hair and the small bit of scalp it exposes. I can see a trace of red in the skin. Then come the vast forehead, her green eyes and Puritan nose. Her nostrils are perfectly symmetrical.

Frank has staggered to the threshold of the living room, looking justifiably proud. If his eyes can focus, I'm sure he'll think he did all this damage. If Anna's eyes can focus, then she, like Julie, will want answers. Anna's expression, though, when the fullness of her head emerges and her chin rests on the cushions, is not unlike Frank's – dazed. Uncertain. She struggles to form words. Her eyes wander the scene.

I fear the worst.

Julie's voice over the phone scratches at the air.

Anna opens her mouth. Her voice *is* angry, but what comes out is this: "Pictures of naked midgets are *NOT* what I had in mind." I smile. For a moment, I'm able to believe in God. Anna sometimes spouts gibberish when she first stirs. It will take her a minute to come around, and by then I'm convinced I'll have figured out a way to explain this, to enlist her help in saving my friend's marriage.

Julie's shouting into the phone again. *Whose voice is that?* I set the phone down on the table. I'm here, I say to Julie, or maybe to Anna, or Frank. Hang on.

Anna and Frank exchange a beautiful glance, the look two aliens might exchange on simultaneously encountering an unfamiliar planet. Trying to piece it all together, and not sure they have the ability. Can I deal with Julie? Not yet.

Frank's emergence has turned out to be premature. Maybe he heard me say Julie's name into the cordless and realized he's going to have to face her. He's headed for the bathroom again.

I think they'll get through this, but you never know. Relationships are so fragile. Each has a fault line that, once cracked, can never be repaired. But you don't always know where it is. Sometimes that's a good thing.

Anna's standing now, rubbing sleep from her eyes, unsteady on her feet. She's wonderful.

I tell Julie: Here, talk to Frank.

I lay the phone down and slide it across my polished floor, past the wreckage, past a baffled Dante, into the bathroom, where I hope Frank will be able to pick it up and say something kind. I'll have to trust them. I've got to go hug Anna, and fill her in. Everything else will have to wait.

Dr. Bliss and the Library of Toast

THE FIRST PROBLEM WAS WOUNDED pride. As a way to lash out against his ex-wife Katrina for giving up on him (congenital inability to see anything through, etc.), Miles signed a two-year lease on the apartment/museum space, moved north, announced and publicized a grand opening before he'd figured out how to fund any of it. In response, Katrina had taken their amicable divorce to the lawyers and vowed to take Miles for everything he (might have) had.

"Need a hand?"

Miles was hauling the old futon mattress up the steps of his would-be museum when he heard the voice from the sidewalk below. The man attached to the voice wore striped pajamas, a maroon bathrobe and bedroom slippers. Sixty-some, he had steely white hair, two-day stubble and a solid body. He looked like he'd worked the trades.

It was a gray mid-April afternoon. True warmth wouldn't come for at least a month. Thirty-year-old Miles wore torn jeans and a sweatshirt stolen from Katrina. Yes, he needed help.

Five minutes later they had the mattress through the door into the stripped-to-studs exhibit space. The man adjusted his bathrobe and took in the surroundings. Electrical bundles and raw wood. A prominent fuse box. Sawdust-smeared windows let in smoky light. They each kept a hand on the mattress while they caught their breath.

"Museum, huh?" Despite his outfit, the man didn't seem daft.

"In three weeks." Miles often had trouble grasping the logistical ramifications of his commitments.

"Good luck."

Five minutes more and they had the futon stuffed up the narrow stairs and centered on the floor of the living space. The single room with kitchenette and three-quarter bath came with the storefront. On a built-in shelf Miles displayed the brushed-steel sign that would become the museum's nameplate:

THE LIBRARY OF TOAST
WUNDERKAMMER • MUSEUM

"Toast," the man said. "Like rye. Whole wheat." He had a face like pulled taffy. Jowls. There was a matter-of-factness to him that Miles liked.

"More or less," Miles said impatiently. He wanted the story behind the pajamas. He nodded toward them. "Nice look."

The robe was plush terry. The pajamas flannel. "Serves its purpose." The man offered his hand. "I'm Tootie Medaglia."

"The embattled mayor?" Miles grinned. "No shit. I heard you were in jail."

Mayor Medaglia wagged a thick finger in the air. "Indictment. We're a long way from jail."

Miles watched the mayor look around the room. Battered boxes labeled "Onion Man #1" and "Onion Man #3." Vintage toasters. A single suitcase.

The mayor had his hands in his bathrobe pockets. "What brought you to town?"

"Economic opportunity."

"Bullshit." Medaglia scratched himself. "I'm gonna take a piss while you decide if you want a conversation."

The truth was more like economic necessity. No marketable skills. No resume. No income, save the diminishing royalties from Asian licensing of Dr. Bliss. Without Katrina to fall back on, there was no safety net.

He wasn't about to tell the mayor any of that. He fetched snack foods from a grocery bag. Wedges of asiago cheese and Triscuits. He spread it out on the futon and sat.

Medaglia settled in across from Miles. "Tell me two things about my town."

"Population 42,281." Miles had facts. He'd done his research. "And it's the home of the 2003 Minor Planet Society Man of the Year."

The mayor chewed a Triscuit. He nodded. Pondered. "You got a day job?"

"No."

"Hmm."

From what Miles remembered from sketchy news stories, the mayor faced more than a dozen counts of bribery. Racketeering. Extortion. Rumors of mafia ties. Even so, he had a loyal following.

Medaglia stared into him. Cool gray eyes. "What do you do?"

Miles pulled a plastic action figure from his pocket. A man, pudgy. Gray hair. Brown corduroys. Lab coat. "Meet Dr. Bliss."

The mayor sat, Buddha in striped flannels, waiting. "And?"

Miles shrugged. "He's big in Japan."

"Okay. What's the shtick?"

"Graphic novels."

A knowing smile. "Sex books?"

Miles shook his head. "Comics." A cold draft blew steadily across the wood floor.

"I don't like comics."

"That's okay. I don't like politicians."

The mayor chomped Triscuits. "Nice."

Miles tucked Dr. Bliss away. "So. You guilty?"

The mayor pulled a steno notebook from his bathrobe pocket. Tossed it onto the mattress. "Make a note: kid's got spunk, but he shouldn't push it."

O

The second problem was Meek, the rock opera composer turned musical playwright, whose unfinished satire "City Hall: The Musical," based on the life and times of Mayor Tootie, had just been accepted into New York's Fringe Festival. Meek needed fast money to stage a production. His odds were good: the announcement had made him the new darling of the local arts scene.

"You know he's a trust fund kid," Medaglia said.

They sat, Miles and the Mayor, in a cramped booth at Otis' Diner. They shared a fondness for rye toast.

"If that was true," Miles said, "he wouldn't need money."

There were only two sources of arts funding in town, patrons Miles had just begun to cultivate. He didn't welcome the sudden competition. His appeal historically rested on a quirky charm and dogged likeability that didn't fare well under deadline pressures or in pithy media sound bites. He'd met Meek on the street a couple times, exchanged pleasantries.

"Parents cut him off after his unfinished rock opera. Three years holed up in a basement for some opus on the life of Martin van fuckin' Buren." Medaglia cast an irritated look at Miles. "Tell me how he gets taken serious."

"Rich kids," Miles said. "Don't get me started."

Across the street, Ralph the hardware manager set up a sidewalk display of gardening tools.

What attention in town wasn't directed at Meek was on Mayor Tootie himself. An iconic figure even before his arrest, his unusual defense strategy had drawn regional media attention. Quirky feature stories. Now trial had been set for May 2. A newspaper sat on the table between them, folded to a Sunday spread: "Trying Times for The Oddfather." TV crews were curious.

"It's a circus," the mayor said. Signature striped pajamas. Soft maroon robe. "I got a city to run."

Miles felt pressure of his own. He needed money for floors, walls and other opening night essentials. He had cash to live a month. Two if he scaled back to Weetabix and peanut butter. The fast-approaching gala had to raise $50k. And Katrina was ratcheting up her assault.

"The latest from the lawyers," Miles said. He picked at generously buttered toast. Strained to keep his voice calm. "I've got a month to demonstrate the museum as an economically viable idea. Otherwise, they say my failure to look for work will be seen as contempt."

The mayor chewed rye. "Contempt. That's funny."

Behind the counter, Otis consolidated coffee from two pots. Ancient and stooped with tight silver curls, he had once, according to local legend, been a noted ad man.

"The cubicle is not a habitat I can survive in," Miles said. "I'm an artist. An improviser. My task is to amuse and inspire. To expand perceptions of the possible. These skills are wasted in the work force. Besides, the last time I had a regular job, I went catatonic within a month."

"Are you finished?" Medaglia slurped black coffee. "I'm twelve days from trial."

"Sorry." Miles chewed toast in silent solidarity. Tried to read the mayor's well-lived face. "You worried?"

"I don't believe in worry." He wiped crumbs from his robe. "I do need to strategize. Offload some tasks. Could use your help."

"Name it."

"Make a few stops for me. Pick up some bets. A small basketball pool."

"You can't be serious."

"I'll cut you in."

Miles leaned forward, spoke in hushed tones. "You're under indictment."

"Lose the drama," the mayor said. "The judge is a customer, for one thing." Through the window, he kept on eye on his town. His disappointment in Miles palpable. "In your position I thought cash might interest you. But don't do anything makes you uncomfortable."

The next day. The mayor's booth at Otis'. Toast and coffee had become an afternoon routine. They perused media coverage. Fine-tuned tactics. There was an article – anecdotes about a petty, vindictive side. How he'd shut down a popular restaurant for overcrowding the night he was turned away by a bouncer who didn't recognize him.

"So fucking what," the mayor said. "So I'm not perfect."

A man approached the booth.

"How quaint. The disgraced mayor and his new lackey." Meek. A rat's nest of butterscotch hair and two-day whiskers. Pressed Brooks Brothers shirt over torn jeans. Ray-Bans. Steam rose from a paper coffee cup in his hands.

"Fuck," Medaglia said to the room. His eyes narrowed on Meek. "How's the hatchet business?"

"Two songs in radio rotation." Meek ran a hand through unkempt hair, as if he were on camera. "It's going to be a hit."

"It's fucking slander. A hack musical revue not fit for summer camp."

"It's a modern gangster musical in neo-swing style."

"Don't be smug with me, you fuck. I'm still the mayor. Cars can get towed, theaters shut down for building violations. Things happen." His face was red. He turned to Miles. "Kid, make a note."

A vein throbbed in Meek's neck. "Are you threatening me?"

The mayor's focus became diffuse. "I'm sorry," he said, louder. "Have we met?"

"Pathetic." Meek shook his head, addressed Miles. "He's tried this act before. He was a city administrator, a small town in Jersey, 20 years ago. Right, Mayor? Got indicted for bribing the police force. He brought evidence he was under psychiatric care, and the charges got dropped. You think people won't see through this?" Meek spun out of the diner.

The mayor sipped coffee and stewed. There were times, Miles had learned already, you didn't interrupt.

Medaglia pushed up the sleeves of his robe. "It's 30 years ago," he said. "Make a note, kid. You're gonna fuck somebody, get your facts right."

They walked Main Street. A warm afternoon. Striped pajamas. No robe.

"So I go out this morning to pick up a toaster," Miles said. "Classic 1947 Universal with spring-loaded doors, a cornerstone of the opening night display – I come back the entire museum is sheetrocked."

Medaglia's leather slippers slapped the sidewalk. "No shit?"

Sun shone on ornate facades and simple shops, a quintessential blend of the upscale and the unimproved that had earned the town kudos in travel mags. The mayor walked slow, chest out. A sense of ownership.

"No shit," Miles said. He squinted against the glare. "Know anything about that?"

"I might."

"You can't *do* that."

Medaglia flashed a radiant smile. "Course I can. I'm the mayor."

Wherever he went, Medaglia worked the crowd. A waved greeting at the window of an insurance agency. Quick handshakes and staccato queries – *how's business, Johnny? Doris well?* Undeniable charm. The flannel-clad boss taken in stride.

They passed the barber shop. The hardware. Ralph's sidewalk display of gardening tools. "Seriously," Miles said. "Is that ethical?"

"A mayor can't worry about etiquette," Medaglia said. "He has to focus. Get things done. Keep the lights on. Collect the trash. The shit nobody wants to think about. At the same time, move the city forward. This requires certain skills. Broker solutions. Consolidate power. A penchant for achieving goals."

"Sounds primitive," Miles said.

"It's called results." Slap, slap went the slippers. The mayor's blunt style appealed to Miles, weary from the constant contortions required of a people pleaser. Slap, slap. "You get the toaster?"

"Eventually. There were complications. I give the woman my credit card – it's an antique store up north –it gets rejected."

"Didn't pay your bill?"

"Worse. Katrina. I've been using a joint account she forgot about." Miles possessed what he saw as a rare ability to remain undaunted in the face of reality. Katrina saw it differently. "My last reliable source of funding. From here on, it's strictly cash. This is a problem." Miles' voice rose half an octave. It happened when he got anxious. "I've got bills. And the clock is ticking."

"Tell me about it."

Miles felt a pang. He tended to forget the mayor could face hard time.

"Relax, kid. Your situation will work out. Meantime, we need to talk defense strategy." Medaglia waited while Miles dug out the steno. "I'm questioning the pajamas," he said. "Too Junior Soprano. On the other hand, a shift in strategy this late could seem calculated. Your thoughts?"

Miles struggled to shift gears. The pajama defense had always seemed flawed to him, but then this wasn't his area of expertise. And there was his general reticence to think beyond his own situation. "I can't do this right now."

The mayor stepped in front of him. Leaned in close. "Come here," he said. With the back of one thick hand, he tapped Miles once on each cheek. "Focus. I need you on the pajamas question."

"Right." Miles flushed, chastised. A little afraid.

Medaglia looked at him, contrite. "Don't make me do that. Friendship's a two-way street."

Around the corner, to a bakery café whose specialty was Russian tea cakes. Broadway-style music played from a speaker under a rose awning.

"Mayor Tootie." A man called from inside. Jovial. "It's your song."

Piano and synthesized strings led a gruff-voiced singer into the chorus: *"Nothing's free in my town..."*

Medaglia's eyes got small. His face reddened.

"Forget it," Miles said. "Let's go."

"You cross me I'll track you down..."

For a long moment, Medaglia stared at the speaker as if its workings, its very existence, were a mystery to him. Then he flung his body through the café's open doorway. Within seconds, the music cut off. Seconds later, a crash Miles hypothesized as a stereo being smashed on a tile floor, and a series of blows not unlike thin metal being thrashed by a blunt object. The red-faced, pajama-clad mayor stormed out and stalked down the street.

Miles struggled to catch up.

Medaglia stared grimly forward. His breathing heavy, carefully even.

They passed the florist.

"As an idea," the mayor said, "it was almost funny. As a fact of life, it's fuckin' problematic."

They passed the pharmacy, in the shade of a storybook maple. Hard breaths.

Miles wasn't sure how to proceed. He tried humor. "How about I pick you up some anger management brochures?"

Medaglia's glare chilled him.

They passed the organic grocery. A full parking lot midafternoon. The mayor had pushed a zoning variance to make it possible.

"What are you gonna do?" Miles asked.

Medaglia raised an eyebrow. His breathing slowed. "What I always do," he said. "Deal with it."

O

The third problem was that Grace liked Meek, a local boy. Of the two arts patrons in town, she was the heavy. No serious project could happen without her. The first had been relatively easy to court. Giovanna C, retired opera singer, local legend, stalwart arts patron. Back in the day, she'd been a favorite at fundraisers for her celebrated high notes, her on-demand ability to crack glass. Once, the story went, she had shattered a garnet gemstone at a society wedding in response to a challenge from the bride's father.

"Is it a library or a museum?" Close-cropped platinum hair. Enormous jeweled earrings. She poured herself brandy from a beveled decanter and looked down on Miles. "Do you lend slices of sourdough? Pumpernickel?"

"The Library of Toast is a concept museum."

She shook her head. "Or a conundrum," she said. "A quaint idiocy."

Miles wagged a finger in the air. "*Wunderkammer,*" he said. He sensed her warm to the German. "The reconnection of art and science. A cabinet of curiosities in the European tradition, with particular focus on neglected scientists, local artists and, of course, the history and provenance of browned bread. A house of wonder, inquiry and performance." Again, he'd hit upon a word that warmed the air. He rolled with it. "Dr. Bliss himself will be there. He has his own comet. Evolving theories about galactic expansion."

Miles had spent the morning working on the Wall of Toasters. Polishing chrome. Sanding shelves. He'd spent $1300 on two prize models thanks to a line of credit the mayor had cosigned. One, a rare Pelouze vertical circa 1912, would be the centerpiece of the exhibition. The other, a 1929 Toastmaster, was an original pop-up model.

"And then there's young Meek." Giovanna held her glass deftly, the brandy untouched. "The Fringe Festival. A locally birthed musical. I have limited funds."

"Unfinished," Miles cut in. "Don't waste your money." Words charged with his resentment of the young and entitled. "He won't deliver. He has a history." Natural selection. Survival of the fastest. "Did I mention performance? Live piano. Maybe you'd grace us with a song. Dr. Bliss is a big fan."

He left with a commitment for $7,500.

"No kidding?" The mayor's booth at Otis'. Medaglia in crisp white shirt and tie. "Nice work."

Miles sipped at bitter midafternoon coffee, unimpressed with his efforts. He'd spent that amount and more already on contractors. His account down to triple digits. "I've got forty-plus still to raise."

Otis wiped the counter.

"Stop with the negatives. Some advice, kid. Be in the solutions business. You'll make more friends." The mayor adjusted his cuffs. The business attire brought out the dock worker in him. "What's your take on the new look?"

Miles frowned. "I liked the pajamas."

"Understood. But sentimentality aside."

"It's good," Miles said. "Smart. What's the strategy?"

Outside, gray and damp.

"I'm not at liberty. We are, however, well situated. Suffice to say."

Miles was afraid to ask for details. He drained his mug. Got a mouthful of grounds. Not wanting to seem soft, he swallowed. Bit into rye, a perfect golden brown. That morning he'd bought Weetabix on sale, a precaution. "I need a money strategy," he said. "The ex is out for my hide. Wants to attach my Japan earnings."

"My third wife hit me in the head with a hot iron."

Miles' brain hurt. "What does that even *mean*?"

"Means stop whining. You got a problem, do something."

"Like what?"

"You want her taken care of, say the words."

A rush. "You serious?"

56

The mayor raised an eyebrow. "Eat your toast. I'm making a point. You want to win, it's balls-out every day. The boy Meek, he's had every fuckin' advantage in life, he's thrown it away."

A draft leaked through the window. Miles chilled even in his sweatshirt. "Fine. But Katrina—"

Medaglia grabbed a napkin, wiped his mouth. "Enough. Was she wrong to want a little security? You made choices, fine. Don't blame her she chose different." He balled the napkin in his fist. "No one wants to hear it, kid. Figure out what you want. Go after it, or don't." He pushed his plate away. "Meantime, we need to discuss the composer fuck." A second song from the musical, "Pucker Up or Get Padlocked," was in heavy rotation on local radio. "Give me one reason I shouldn't have him whacked."

Miles chose to interpret this as banter, the mayor's way of blowing off steam. "Two words," he said. "Defense strategy."

"Fair enough."

"Besides, a violent end would only add to his cachet. Better to discredit him."

The mayor's brow furrowed. "It's good you're not in my line of work. You lack a certain directness." He leaned back in the booth. "Go raise money."

Grace was a tougher nut to crack. She ran a café. There was family money, and a local real estate empire she'd built herself. She had renovated the local movie theater into a performance space she'd opened with a Romanian trapeze act. She had grand vision, a commitment to local art, and no love for the mayor.

"He's a gangster," she said. "An embarrassment." She gestured at the newspaper open on the counter. Miles didn't need to look. An interview with Meek in the local arts weekly. Promoting the show and poking at the mayor. Including the anecdote about the New Jersey indictment. "A shift in public opinion," Medaglia had said. "This I can't have. I blame the boy Meek. We need a solution."

With Grace, Miles avoided the character issue and merely pitched his idea.

"Sorry," she told him, a trace of East Europe in her voice. "I like it. But I've got a theater to book." Soft-bodied, slightly pear-shaped, she wore small glasses on a cord around her neck. Her eyes told him she enjoyed being entertained but had little tolerance for bullshit. She'd slated Meek's musical for a three-week run post-Fringe.

"The musical's a disaster," Miles said. "Have you heard it?"

"Don't go there," she said. "It's cheap."

Local art adorned the walls. Watercolors. The café was immaculate and, at this late afternoon hour, empty. Miles sipped a latté, a rare treat. Seen a certain way, things didn't look good. He was two payments behind with informally agreed-on alimony. Plus sales of Dr. Bliss, year to date, showed sharp decline.

"The show's cheap," he said. Desperation spawning a degree of honesty. "It's obvious. Shooting fish."

"It's edgy. Timely. Local." An adversarial tone. "It's going to do great." She eyed her cell phone. "I'm a business woman. You want to compare return on investment?"

"You're an arts patron," Miles countered. "Invest in possibility."

Grace smiled. "Not bad. Still, I'm committed to Meek."

"You're telling me you can't do both?"

"Not can't." She picked up her phone. Glanced at the screen. "Here's how this looks. You come to town thinking you can hoodwink the locals, steal funding from a hometown boy."

"What can I do to convince you?"

"Teach me something about my town."

Miles sensed an opening. His confidence soared. "Tell you what," he said. "Don't write a check today."

Grace laughed. A good laugh, full-throated.

"Come to the opening. If you're not sold, keep your money."

O

The fourth problem was Dr. Bliss.

"I need you to become an artist again." Miles paced the hay loft in the workshop of his friend and aging mentor, Donal Worsham. "One night. A performance piece, grand and elliptical. We'll incorporate your discoveries, but also your writings. Your music. Your art."

Worsham had a colorful history. His first career as a surrealist painter. Hard-bop pianist of some repute, then years teaching music to suburban high school kids. Essayist on environmental issues. Three years earlier he had discovered a small, irregular comet which now bore his name. He'd been the Minor Planet Society's Man of the Year. Miles his "date" at the gala, Worsham decked out in short lab coat, fuzzy green sweater and brown cords – the birth of Dr. Bliss. The Carnegie Planet Search Team had since disputed the comet's authenticity and Worsham, a fragile soul, had retreated into development of an obscure theory about rates and methods of galactic expansion. Of late, he seemed disheartened at a lack of continuity in his life and work.

"No, no, and no," he said. Bic pens in the pocket of his lab coat.

"You're a renaissance man," Miles reminded Worsham. A telescope perched in the bay, aimed out the loft doors. Painted styrofoam balls of various sizes hung on fishing wire from massive wood beams, cotton fluff strung between them. Below, on the ground floor, two easels, a desk with a manual typewriter, and a John Deere bucket tractor circa 1950. "You're the primary reason I came to this valley."

"Economic opportunity, Miles, is the reason you came here. A thriving community of fellow freaks where the cost of living is low and the coffee shops upscale."

"Nevertheless," Miles said. "There were other locations."

"I've wanted to talk with you. It was endearing at first, this Dr. Bliss. But I walk into a store and see an action figure, a comic character, wearing my trousers. How do I feel."

"Not a comic character. A hero. You're the inspiration. The muse. You'll always be Dr. Bliss. And besides, I've promised."

Worsham shook his head.

"Don't say no. Consider. An opportunity at synergy. A career-making statement."

Worsham studied his model of the spheres, stern. "You put me out there, your trained seal. Have mercy. Leave me alone."

Miles felt a pang but pushed it aside. "Please. I need you."

"You mock me."

"I honor you."

Worsham stared out at the night sky. "I won't give away my dignity. The answer is no."

The next day, at Otis'. Miles slid into the booth, slid a check in front of Medaglia. His first piece of real mail at the museum had come that morning, from the city. "What's this?" he asked.

"I put you on the payroll."

"But I don't do anything."

"Bullshit. We're doing something now." Medaglia signaled Otis, rye toast for two. "Flip through that notebook of yours. How much of it is things I've told you to write down."

While it was true the mayor's instructions had come to dominate Miles' notes, he thought he'd been gathering info on the sly, fodder for a new graphic novel.

"Are you adding to the city's cultural landscape? Are you consulting – informally – on how to bash the brains of that musical trust fund fuck?"

Miles shook his head. "I don't know."

Medaglia pushed the check away. "Donate it to charity. Maybe a museum." He sipped coffee. "Case closed. What's next?"

The case wasn't closed, but it was pointless butting heads with the mayor, and Miles did have other topics. "Dr. Bliss," he said. "The opening. What am I gonna do?"

Their toast arrived. "Threats? Bribes? There's gotta be something."

"He doesn't care about money. And he's too disheartened to fear anything."

"Where's his vulnerability?"

Miles thought. "Ego. A sense of legacy."

"There you go. That's how we hook him." Medaglia chewed toast. He wore a white shirt and gold tie. "By the way, I'm taking care of our friend Meek."

Miles wary. "What do you mean?"

"There's a story he bought off a girl upstate to dodge a date rape charge in college."

"That's not true."

"It is if I make it true."

"No." Miles sipped water. His throat dry. "I don't want any part of that."

"Don't be squeamish," the mayor said. "Besides, this was your idea. Discredit, you said. Fine. Done. Next."

"No," Miles said. "Not next."

"Okay." The mayor's eyes steel. "What's your solution?" He raised an eyebrow and stared at Miles until he blushed. "That's what I thought."

Miles watched his water glass sweat.

"One thing about life, kid. You can't leave the house without getting your hands dirty." The stare continued, unthreatening, insistent. "This helps you, I might point out."

Miles squirmed in his seat. *This is the way the world works,* he told himself. *It was only a rumor. Meek would recover.*

"Focus," the mayor said. "This Dr. Bliss. He leave the house if your life is in danger?"

Miles made the shift, grateful. Played out the possibility in his head. "Probably not."

"Okay. What does get him out?"

Again, Miles considered. The truth mattered here. "A ruse that strokes his ego."

"Good." Medaglia smiled. "We'll work on that. Meantime, walk with me. I've got a meeting."

He left ten on a five-forty tab and they headed toward Town Hall. Outside the hardware, Medaglia stopped to slap Ralph the manager's shoulder as he replenished his display of garden tools – rakes, hoes, half-length shovels. They nearly got mowed down by Meek, coming out of the store with a small paper bag in hand. The vein in his neck began to throb when he recognized the mayor.

"You're a fucking scourge," he said. Butterscotch hair moussed into a just-woke-up wave. "A parasite. And you," he said to Miles. "Character smears. False accusations."

"I'm not proud of that," Miles acknowledged.

"Shut up, kid," the mayor said. "We have no idea what you're talking about."

"You're a thug and you're going to prison." Meek's voice trembled. The vein in his neck played a techno beat, but Miles gave him grudging respect for his balls.

The mayor reached out his arms to the town. "I can't go to jail. I'm too important to the local economy."

Meek took a breath. Another. He turned his focus to Miles. "Did you know your friend was once convicted of assaulting a man with a lit cigarette, an ashtray and a fireplace log? Ask him about that."

Miles looked to the mayor.

"Charged, not convicted," Medaglia said. "That was a painful time in my life. I don't want to talk about it." He nodded his chin at Meek. "Come here, fuck. Lean in close." Meek did. "Let me tell you something. One phone call, you don't wake up tomorrow morning. You think about how far you want to take this."

Nose to nose on the sidewalk. Miles and Ralph awkward spectators. Meek mastered himself and managed a sly grin. "You haven't asked about the show," he said. "I've just finished the anthem. 'Marry Your Enemies and Fuck Your Friends.'"

It was too much for the mayor. He grabbed a shovel from the hardware display and swung. Meek ducked, a young man's fast reflexes. Red-faced Medaglia wound up to swing again. Meek ran easily across Main Street, laughing. The mayor spun, hurled the shovel after him. It soared overhead, a giant boomerang, narrowly missing the composer but scoring a direct hit on the plate glass window of Arthur's Barber Shop, which shattered spectacularly. Shards rained on sidewalk and street.

Stunned silence. The mayor stood hands on hips, breathing hard. Ralph and Miles flanked him. Through the space where the window had been, Arthur and a half-shaved customer watched, doe-eyed.

Medaglia was the first to find words. "Arthur," he called. He flashed a thumbs-up at the barber. "We'll take care of this. Pronto." He watched Meek's disappearing figure. Addressed Miles. "He stole my line. Can't I sue his ass?"

Miles at his elbow, steno in hand.

"Make a note, kid. A new window for Arthur's shop."

O

The opening came tantalizingly close to solving all Miles' problems.

Giovanna sang, and though no longer capable of breaking glass, she was still potent. The town turned out in force, intrigued by Miles's quirky concept. The Wall of Toasters was a hit, an irresistible display of vintage chrome on staggered shelves. A contemporary Cuisinart anchored a snack station featuring homemade jams, and breads from a local baker labeled for the occasion with the Dewey Decimal System. Dr. Bliss made an appearance, in full uniform. His terms: he wouldn't speak. Played jazz piano on an old upright at the center of the room. Miles surrounded him with an improvised tribute to

Worsham's work and a promise that an expanded, formalized version of same would bump Onion Man as the *wunderkammer*'s first full show. The tribute, mounted humbly on a series of cubicle dividers, illustrated Worsham's work on galactic expansion and summarized his challenge to Kepler's laws of planetary motion.

"Fascinating." A stooped figure lingered inches from the Worsham boards, peering through half-glasses. Miles almost didn't recognize Otis.

"How so?"

On the piano, a bluesy version of Ellington's "I Got it Bad."

"The possibility that both gravitational and anti-gravitational phenomena may result from the same type of energy," Otis said.

"Exactly," Miles improvised. "And did you know that the rate of the universe's expansion is roughly equivalent to one piece of toast per year?"

Otis nodded vaguely and moved on.

Miles had provided multiple opportunities for philanthropy. A donations box. A call for membership in Dr. Bliss' Galactic Expansion Club. His museum coming to life.

They even survived a performance of Meek's would-be show-stopper "It's Only a Crime if You Get Caught." Miles had invited him both as a way to woo Grace and an attempt to right his Karmic balance.

Medaglia, days from trial, arrived with gauze wrapped around his head, the result of a vigilante attack at a Town Council meeting two nights before. An enraged citizen with a handgun. A shot that grazed his ear and made national news.

Miles embraced him. The mayor tapped his heart to acknowledge the concern. Fingered his injured lobe. "Guy was fuckin' unhinged. Parking tickets. You believe that? Certain individuals, I could understand the anger, but not this guy. Lucky he's a bad shot."

"But the timing," Miles said. "How's this look?"

The mayor leaned in, spoke confidentially. "Fuckin' fantastic," he said. "Public sympathy swings my way, at the perfect time." There was a bruise below his right eye. He winked it anyway. "Clean living." Across the room, Meek mingled with Giovanna's entourage. "Meantime, seems I overestimated the chastity of the arts community," Medaglia said. The trumped-up date rape story had backfired, resulting only in increased publicity for Meek. "Anything short of caught with his dick in a local hole is just colorful bio. So we take a new approach. You've set the tone. We embrace the fuck. I offer to perform the lead role at a preview. You'll write up some talk points."

Grace came with her checkbook. "Impressive," she said. Even in a cocktail dress she was a daunting figure.

"It's coming along," Miles said. "Next up is the Path of Petrified Toast. I'm experimenting with various glazes. Varnishes."

At the piano, Worsham launched into "But Not For Me." Grace nodded in his direction. "So this is your Dr. Bliss."

"Local resident," Miles crowed. "Former Minor Planet Society Man of the Year."

She nodded, acknowledging the point. "He seems ambivalent about his role."

Miles winced. "He's a conflicted individual."

"I know. I talked with him."

Shit.

Grace measured him with her eyes. It unnerved him. "You just make it up as you go, don't you?"

"Pretty much," he admitted.

Side by side, they watched Worsham.

"There are rumors that date rape smear about Meek traces back to you," she said. "I'd be disappointed if that proved true."

Dr. Bliss played piano to a packed room. The mayor, beaming, worked the crowd.

"So would I," he told her. A part of him felt ashamed. Another part proud of his pluck. He didn't know how to reconcile the two.

Fuck it. Why try. "Look. My wife left me. I sleep on the floor of my unfunded museum. Dr. Bliss is all I've got." He had her attention. "I wish I was nobler. More serious. It's not in me. I go for tragedy, it comes out a comic book." He had no idea where this was going. "But I like the town. I like the mayor. I might even grow to like Meek. And if you fund this thing, I'll try to do it right. Involve the community. Listen to ideas." He shrugged. "Either way, I'm staying. I'll make it work."

Dr. Bliss eased into "Good Morning, Heartache."

"Here's what I'm going to do," Grace said. Again with the eyes. "I'm going to leave a check in that basket." She indicated the wicker atop the upright. "But I'm going to let your friend decide the amount."

She walked to the piano. Sat next to Worsham on the bench. Spoke into his ear as he played. Worsham spoke briefly back. She wrote a check, placed it in the wicker basket, and left.

Miles felt he should be worried. He wasn't. The check might have one zero or four. It didn't matter. He was viable, at least for tonight. He parked next to Worsham, who gave him a look that said, *Dr. Bliss Galactic Expansion Club? You should be ashamed.* Miles shrugged in a way that said, *Look, I meant it. You're a hero to me.* He wasn't even tempted to look at the check. He rested his head on Worsham's shoulder for a few measures, then sought out the mayor.

"A fine party, kid." Medaglia wrapped an arm around him. Traces of dried blood showed through his bandaging. "Did Grace come through?"

"I have no idea. But never mind that now." They strolled the party's periphery while Miles talked. "Comic Con is coming up and I've got the next Dr. Bliss book."

"What about the evil ex-wife?"

Worsham slowed the tune to a dirge, took it to the bridge with a touch so soft it made the keys cry.

"Forget the ex-wife," Miles said. "Think Norway. They're crazy for comics. Dr. Bliss gets a Norwegian sidekick and presto – licensing deal. It'll be months before Katrina learns of it."

The mayor nodded. "Not bad. So what's the story?"

"Dr. Bliss and the Mafioso Mayor," he said. "In which our hero exposes an evil industrialist whose plant's chemical runoff has tainted the local water supply. The town's embattled mayor, about to be tried for corruption, orders a cleanup." He told Medaglia the basics. "At the City Council meeting, when the mayor makes an impassioned plea against the offending company, the industrialist shoots him in the head."

Medaglia frowned. "I don't like that."

"Wait," Miles said. "The bullet only grazes him, and a week later, when the mayor shows up for his arraignment, he says –"

Medaglia jumped in. "*If a bullet in the head didn't stop me, neither will these trumped-up charges.*"

Miles beamed. "Yes!"

"One thing," said the mayor. "The title's gotta change. I don't like that word. It's degrading."

"No problem," said Miles. "We'll work that out. Meantime, let me introduce you to Dr. Bliss."

Strange Trajectory: A Story Of Phineas Gage

WAIVING THE CLAIMS OF personal and private affection, with a magnanimity more than praiseworthy, the mother and friends, at my request have cheerfully placed this skull (which I now show you) in my hands, for the benefit of science. It is regretted that no autopsy could have been had, so that the precise condition of the encephalon at the time of his death might have been known. [1]

September 13, 1848. A morning like any other, as far as Phineas Gage was concerned. Vermont sun still warm, but a hint of fall in the air. The quiet, steady rhythm. The grunts of men laboring, the sounds of hammer hitting spike, of heavy rails carried and dropped on rocky ground. The sporadic, idle conversation. Phineas at 25, strong and healthy, a construction foreman for the Rutland and Burlington Railroad. A man with hopes of advancement.

Phineas had no way of knowing that this day was special, that he was about to make history. That his "case" would be the subject of scientific discussion more than a hundred years after his death. That his brain would one day be electronically reconstructed on a computer screen, scrutinized from every possible angle. Phineas was simply doing his job on a sunny Vermont day, with the air just beginning to turn.

Phineas worked slowly that morning. Methodically. To lay rail across Vermont, it was necessary to level the terrain by controlled blasting. Among other tasks, Phineas was in charge of the detonations. The procedure ingrained in him. Drill holes in the granite. Fill the holes with blasting powder. Plant a fuse, cover with sand and tamp with the iron to compress it all. Trigger an explosion into the rock.

The tamping rod measured three and a half feet long, an inch and a quarter in diameter. Twenty-two pounds, seven ounces. A single long cut of iron, straight and worn smooth from handling. Fine-pointed at one end, rounded at the other. Within an hour of beginning the morning's work, it would create a sweat in Phineas' hands, which were callused all along the pads of the palms. By noon each day, it would feel like an extension of his arms, the weight forgotten, absorbed into the rhythm of the procedure, which he would repeat ten, twelve, twenty times a day. To clear rock. To lay track. Phineas loved the work. The fact that his labor was producing something worthwhile, connecting Rutland and Burlington to the great cities of the northeast. With every blast, every stroke of his tamping iron, Phineas felt the future moving northward through Vermont, felt part of something larger than himself.

Behind him, his crew loaded rock upon a platform car with a derrick. Phineas prepared a blast while the men cleared the last one behind and beneath him.

"The preacher said it was a sin. It's true. He said the child is sinful." Henry's voice rose with the effort of landing heavy stone into the bucket.

Phineas scratched at a hole in the rock, making space to lay a fuse. When all this was finished, when the railroad was built, he would move to Burlington. Run the repair yard. Find a woman who understood his ambition.

Beneath the granite shelf where Phineas stood, Thomas scratched his head. "But the child's an idiot. It's not a choice he makes."

"Did you fellows know Thomas was a philosopher?"

Laughter.

Thomas and Henry loaded stone, the bucket at the end of a long rope. They signaled to Arthur, who pulled on the end of the rope with Bart to hoist the stone. Stack it in an ox cart and haul it away.

"Five years old and can't speak to be understood. It's God's punishment. That's what the preacher said, and that's what I believe."

ANGLE: Based on measurements of the iron rod and on the recorded descriptions of the accident, we determined the range of likely trajectories. We simulated those trajectories in three-dimensional space. We modeled the rod's trajectory as a straight line connecting the center of the entry hole at orbital level to the center of the exit hole. This line was then carried downward to the level of the mandibular ramus. The skull anatomy allowed us to consider entry points within a 1.5 cm radius. The trajectory connecting each of the entry and exit points was tested at multiple anatomical levels. Acceptable trajectories were those which, at each level, did not violate certain conditions.

Behind Phineas, behind his crew, two flatcars pulled by dust-colored horses moved up on the last finished rails. There the ties went down, five to a twenty-eight-foot length of rail.

"Heave!"

Iron men, five to a rail on each side of the track, pulled on command, hefted the six-hundred pound iron forward, dropped it in place at the word "Down!" and lined it to the gauge.

"What does Sarah think?" Thomas wiped sweat from his brow, leaving a residue of granite dust.

The little car was already moving forward while clampers and spikers fastened down the rail.

"She thinks he's her son." Henry leaned against the platform car, legs crossed in dusty black work pants.

Phineas tamping. Smooth, even strokes. Each stroke connecting him to the future, to the new nation that will emerge.

Thomas, hands on hips, squinting into sun. "But what does she *say?*"

Closer by. Muscles moving rock.

"She says he's her son."

The clang of hammer against spike. The lingering smell of sulfur.

Thomas adjusted his cap. "What would you say?"

Phineas poured sand.

"Well?"

"Come on," said Henry, loading rock. "We're falling behind."

Thomas stood his ground. "What would you say?" Nothing.

"He barks. Growls. Like an animal," Thomas says. Behind them, the grunts of men loading rail onto a flatcar. "I'm just saying. The mouth speaks the expression of the soul."

Phineas shook his head. "The things you all find to talk about."

"Well," said Thomas. "What do you think, Phineas?"

"I'll not speculate on His ways. It's blasphemy."

Henry's hand lingered on a chunk of granite. "I don't know what's God's punishment," he said. "I know about taking care of your own. Right, Phineas?"

Thomas laughed. "Don't ask him about family. He's busy building the great railroad. Can't remember who his family is. Where they live."

"Enough," said Phineas. He drew a match from a leather pouch around his waist. "Take cover."

ANGLE: Only seven trajectories satisfied all conditions. Two of those seven were rejected as anatomically improbable because they would not have been compatible with survival (the resulting massive infection would not have been controllable in the pre-antibiotic era). When checked in our collection of normal brains, one of the remaining five trajectories spared language and motor functions but fit the hole in the skull, and was thus chosen as the most likely trajectory.

Phineas wasn't dreaming about the future. He wasn't dulled by the effects of whiskey. It was just a moment, something he couldn't have identified even if it had occurred to him. Maybe a sound from one of the other crews, maybe as simple as a cloud crossing the sun, a passing shadow to take Phineas' eye momentarily away, to make him lose his rhythm, his sense of timing, to take his eye off the hole where sand didn't quite guard the powder and the fuse, to prepare for the explosion.

The rod shot out of the hole. A three-and-a-half foot long bullet. A spike into the brain of Phineas Gage. Into his face, just under his left cheek. Up behind his left eye. Through face, brain, skull, then out into sky. Picture the rod emerging from the skull of Phineas Gage, sailing through Vermont air. The tamping rod landed nearly twenty yards away. Phineas landed on his tailbone. Momentarily stunned. (That's how his doctor, John Harlow, later described it in a presentation for the Harvard Medical Society. *Gage was momentarily stunned.*)

Gage said nothing. He held a hand to his face. His men had dived for cover, and raised themselves up fully expecting to see their foreman dead. Phineas tried to get to his feet, and fell back onto the dirt. Shattered rock and sand surrounded him. By now eight or ten men formed a circle around him. He was aware of silence despite a horrible ringing in his ears. A breeze stirred the air. A warm flow of blood from somewhere.

Gage uttered a nervous laugh. "Think I'll need some help getting up."

Henry put a hand under Phineas' shoulder and pulled him up. Blood flowed to the ground. Washed Henry's hands. No one wanted to express what they were thinking. Thomas, though, was the most surprised, who had caught a glimpse before ducking, had seen the start of the explosion. His mind's eye had traced the arc. And Gage's movement, the very fact of his being alive, made Thomas doubt what his eyes had seen. Couldn't have gone through his *skull*. Emerged from his head and shot into September sky.

"We'll need a doctor," someone said.

Someone else asked, "Can you walk?"

Gage staggered a little. Hands moved under him for support. His head felt dizzy. The ground shifted under him. He vomited blood. His legs wobbled like those of a child and he could feel an ache coming from his face. But he concentrated on walking, on the help of the men around him. Blood poured from his head. A river down his back. Down his throat into his stomach. The men carried him in their arms to the road, to the ox cart, a bed strewn with shards of stone, splinters of rough wood, and he rode the three-quarters of a mile to Leicester Junction. They got him to his hotel, to his upstairs room, and sent for a doctor.

ANGLE: There was no damage outside of the frontal lobes. The white matter core was more extensively damaged in the left hemisphere than in the right. Thus, Gage fits a neuroanatomical pattern that we have identified to date in 16 patients within a group of 28 individuals with frontal damage. Their ability to make rational decisions in personal and social matters is invariably compromised and so is their processing of emotion.

The 13th, $7^1/_2$ o'clock, P.M. The small pieces of bone having been taken away, a portion of the brain, an ounce or more, which protruded, was removed, the larger pieces of bone replaced, the edges of the soft parts approximated as nearly as possible, and over all a wet compress, night cap and roller.

Fragments of memory appeared. Pain seared his head. Rock exploded behind closed eyelids. He ducked without moving. Couldn't tell if he was waking or sleeping. If his room was dark or light. Vomited blood. Opened his eyes. A man in the room. A doctor.

Phineas pointed to the hole in his cheek. "The iron entered there and passed through my head," he said.

The doctor sat on a stool, a long distance away. The room looked different, larger, its contours strange. Swollen.

"I hope I'm not much hurt," said Phineas.

The edges of the scalp were everted and the frontal bone extensively fractured, leaving an irregular oblong opening in the skull of two by three and one-half inches. The face, hands and arms were deeply burned.

Blood. Pulse 60, soft and regular.

The doctor, John Harlow, examined and dressed the wounds, laying strips of wet cloth, replacing bits of skin that could be refolded. He worked silently. He couldn't believe Phineas was alive. The doctor was young, an avid reader, a follower of medical developments. He'd seen nothing like this. Who had? As he worked, his amazement grew. Blood everywhere. Phineas sat, composed, talking. The doctor didn't know what to say, so he said nothing.

The globe of the left eye was protruded from its orbit by one-half its diameter, and the left side of the face was more prominent than the right side. The pulsations of the brain were distinctly seen and felt.

The hands and arms were dressed, the head elevated, the wound in the cheek left open. Two attendants watched Phineas, to keep him in that position. He slept a little.

At ten o'clock, Dr. Harlow returned. The dressings were saturated with blood. The hemorrhaging had slowed. Pulse 65.

"I don't wish to see the fellows just now," Phineas said. "I'll be back at work in a few days. See them then."

Dr. Harlow removed the stained dressings. Washed the wounds. Passed the index finger of his right hand into the opening in the brain. Checked for foreign bodies. Put on a new compress. Work carefully. This is a case that could make a career.

Phineas saw two Dr. Harlows, or not quite two. Harlow as Siamese twins. Couldn't pull them together in his vision. Couldn't separate them.

"We've done what we can," the doctor said, his first words to Phineas. "Try to rest."

Sept. 14, 7 am. Has slept some during the night. Appears to be in pain. Tumefaction of face considerable, and increasing.

"How did you rest?"

Phineas opened his mouth. No words came. He heard his doctor as if from a great distance, as if through water. He saw shapes. The effort to concentrate too great.

Later. Eyes open? Two new faces in the room. "Mother? Uncle?"

"Yes, Phineas." Harlow's voice. But where was he? "They've come to visit."

"My pants, please." Faces indistinct. Hands fidgeting.

Harlow's voice. "I don't think you..."

"MY PANTS!"

Dr. Harlow handed Phineas the pants.

"Why did you let them in? I don't wish to see anyone." A wave of nausea passed through him. A distant sense of shame. Because he had walked out, he couldn't need them. Couldn't allow it.

The touch of his mother's hand in his. His withdrawing. "You'll come home soon, for a visit. I'll take care of you."

Bleeding into mouth continues.

Phineas hearing the blast. Smelling sulfur. The rhythm of his days moving through his arms. The steady tamping motion. "Who is the foreman in the pit now? Who are they using?"

Sept. 15. Decidedly delirious. A metallic probe passed into the opening at the top of the head, down until it reached the base of the skull, without resistance or pain. Brain not sensitive.

ANGLE: The case of Phineas Gage has fascinated researchers for more than 100 years. For decades, it was an enigma presented to neurology students as a freak story. In this century, as new cases of damage to frontal cortices were delineated, and as frontal lobe function remained [arguably] the least understood aspect of the human brain, Gage gradually acquired landmark status. Only recently, through the emergence of sophisticated brain-imaging technology, have we been able to fully explore this case.

16th. An abundant foetid, sanious discharge from the head with particles of brain matter intermingled, finding its way out from the opening in the top of the head, and also from the one in the base of the skull into the mouth.

Three times a day, Dr. Harlow dressed the head. Ice water was continually kept on the head and face. Attendants carefully cleaned off discharge, externally. Washed the mouth and fauces as often as necessary, with water and disinfecting solutions. The opening in the top of the head covered with oiled silk underneath wet compresses. Phineas stirred, thrashed in bed. Threw his hands and feet about. Head very hot. "I shall not live long this way," he said.

Sept. 23. At this date, ten days after the injury, vision of the left eye, though quite indistinct before, was totally lost. The scalp was reshaven and the edges of the wound brought into apposition as nearly as possible. The discharge less in quantity. Up to this time it had not occurred to me that it was possible for Gage to recover.

Dr. Harlow wadded up saturated bandaging, looked at his patient, prone upon the bed. "There," he said.
Phineas had difficulty raising his head from the pillow. Heard a voice saying, "God's punishment." Sat up. To Dr. Harlow: "What?"

"I didn't say anything."

Outside, steel gray sky. In the distance, an explosion. Granite fragments sailing through autumn air. Rail moving north.

Phineas rolled onto his side, pushed himself upright. Dr. Harlow wiped residue from the table with a towel. Arranged instruments in his bag. It was hard for him to watch Phineas.

"How soon do you think I'll be ready to go back?"

The doctor held a towel in his left hand. Rubbed his fingers back and forth, wiping a probe. Outside, a carriage rattled along the street.

"How much longer?"

The instrument dropped into the bag with a sharp click. "Maybe you should think about a change." The towel draped neatly over the back of a chair. "Something less demanding, physically."

Dizziness. Periodically, Phineas was aware that the ringing in his ears had never fully stopped. "No." Looked at Harlow through his good eye. "Work defines a man." The room shifted. "What would you do if you couldn't see patients?"

Explosion. In his head? Phineas on his knees. A voice. Henry's? *The child is sinful.*

Dr. Harlow moved to him, lips pursed in marginally concealed distaste. Reached down.

Phineas slapped at the hand offered to him. "NO," he said. "I don't need your help." The feel of the iron through his arms.

The hand remained. Sunlight golden on a chair beside him. Dizzy. He took the hand, pulled himself up along the doctor's arm, held himself upright by gripping Dr. Harlow's biceps. Got his balance. Their eyes met for a moment, inches apart, and Phineas found himself using his arms, exerting force, upsetting the doctor's balance.

Harlow released his grip, pulled away. "I'll not wrestle with you."

Phineas outside himself, watching. "See that you don't."

Says he feels comfortable. Appears demented, or in a state of mental lethargy.

"What day is today?"

"Tuesday."

"What time?"

"Morning. Late morning."

Describe the house you grew up in. Count to fifty. Recite the names of the states.

Phineas dutifully responding, trying to focus on the world outside his window.

Discharge from the openings profuse and foetid. Erysipelatous blush on skin of left side of face and head.

Occasional sounds, the slow grind of wagon wheels on road, the voices of people in the streets. Three strokes to the spike. Ten spikes to a rail. Ahead of it all, making it possible for rail to move north.

"Henry and Thomas visited. Yesterday?"

"Yes." Dr. Harlow on his stool, across the room. "Was it good to see them?"

Outside the windows, the cry of a child.

Phineas lied.

"Yes."

Not a lie, maybe. But a look in the faces of the men he worked with. Something in their eyes when they saw him. What it was to be condemned. The thought formed tentatively in Phineas' brain, but there was too much in the way for him to get at it: pain, dizziness, the confines of his room his world, the impossibility of describing how it felt to be Phineas with a hole in his head. Whiting. Salisbury. Cornwall. Towns to be connected.

Harlow writing on a sheet of paper.

"What are you writing?"

"Your case is unusual. I want to keep a record."

Today he appears stronger and more rational than before; calls for food.

ANGLE: Because he survived the momentous injury and his subsequent behavior had been traced, the case held clues to the exploration and mapping of the frontal cortices. It occurred to us that image processing techniques could be used to test this idea by going back in time, reconstituting the accident, and determining the probable placement of his lesion. Our own interest in the case grew out of the idea that Gage exemplified a particular type of cognitive and behavioral defect caused by damage to ventral and medial sectors of prefrontal cortex.

The improvement, however, was short lived. In the night following, he became stupid, did not speak unless aroused, and then only with difficulty; the integuements between the lower edge of the fracture in frontal bone and left nasal protuberance, swollen, hot and red. Failing strength.

What did I do? he wondered. Catalogued past behavior. Found nothing worthy of condemnation.

A picture in Phineas' brain. Rod shooting through skull, into sky. Phineas on the ground, seated, bleeding, looking, marveling. Phineas reaching around him, unable to see for all the blood, feeling around him for whatever he may have lost, trying to locate pieces.

During the three succeeding days the coma deepened. The globe of the left eye became more protuberant, with fungus pushing out rapidly from the internal canthus. Also large fungi pushing up rapidly from the wounded brain, and coming out the opening in the top of the head.

Explosions of light and color and pain, pain so deep it was beautiful. Violet. Cyan. A picture: Phineas, rod in hand, face enraged, swinging at stone, at ox cart, at Harlow, at anyone who is healthy, who does not have a hole in his head.

Pulse 84. Will not take nourishment unless strongly urged. Calls for nothing. Surface and extremities incline to be cool. Friends and attendants are in hourly expectancy of his death, have coffin and clothes in readiness.

No pictures. Only thoughts. That one could feel one's approaching death, one's fading life. That his mother had taught him, as a boy, that emotions reside in the kidney, that doubt resides in the lungs. Thoughts came slowly, in single file, like mourners. What about the soul? Where does the soul reside?

With a pair of curved scissors I cut off the fungi which were sprouting out from the top of the brain and filling the opening, and made free application of caustic to them. With a scalpel I laid open the integuements, between the opening and the roots of the nose, and immediately there were discharged eight ounces of ill-conditioned pus, with blood, and excessively foetid. Tumefaction of left side of face increased. Globe of left eye very prominent.

The railroad moved toward Cornwall. The laying of track. The fastening of ties. Three strokes to a spike, ten spikes to a rail. Four hundred rails to a mile. Sound carried into sky. Miles ahead, surveying parties: a chief engineer, assistant, rodmen, flagmen and chainmen, axemen and teamsters. Henry had become foreman, until Phineas returned. Phineas had become a superstition. A presence as they went about their work. A fear in the back of their minds. They received daily reports of his progress. It was a way of measuring time, like the moving north of steel rail.

Sept. 28 to Oct. 6. Discharge from the openings very profuse and foetid. Pulse ranging from 80 to 96. Speaks only when spoken to. Swallows well, and takes considerable nourishment, with brandy and milk. Says he has no pain.

ANGLE: Dr. Harlow's two papers argued that the case had much to tell about human brain function. This was a period when neurologists had begun to assert that the brain has regions specialized for language movement and perception. Dr. Harlow and [a few] others of his time felt there might also be a region specialized for rational behavior. Lacking proof of exactly where in the brain the lesion was located, however, he could not convince his opponents. His arguments were dismissed as outrageous. These things, it was argued, were the province of religion.

October 6th. Twenty-three days after the injury. General appearance somewhat improved. Pulse 90, and regular. More wakeful. Swelling of left side of face abating. Openings discharging laudable pus profusely.

    Dr. Harlow on his stool. Sunlight and sound through the window. Phineas raised his head.

"How do you feel?"

    How to say. Pain the orange of marigolds. The blue of full moon sky.

"Better."

"Do you remember?"

"I was injured on September 13th. The tamping iron entered here." Phineas pointing to the hole in his cheek. "I struck with the iron. The wrong spot. Could I have my pants?"

    Harlow shifts on his stool. "Your condition won't allow"

Oct. 15th – thirty-second day – Progressing favorably. Fungi disappearing; discharging laudable pus from openings. Takes more food, sleeps well, and says he shall soon go home to visit.

    Dr. Harlow would change the bandages twice a day, and check for healing. Thirty-nine days to form a layer of rubbery tissue across much of the area, to shrink the hole to half its original size. Every morning and every evening new bandages. New conversations. *When were you born? Describe the house you grew up in.*

"I'd like to get back to work."

"Patience. You're not even ready to go for a walk yet."

Explosions of light and sound inside Phineas' head. Some days once, or twice. Some days an unending pyrotechnic display.

Harlow cleaning instruments. Wiping counters. Fingers always rubbing. "Recovery will take a long time. Adjustment to new circumstances." But Phineas suspected something else. Something darker. A recurring dream, his fingers reaching, his mind convinced. What was lost.

Harlow rubbing. "I have to be away for a few days."

"It's okay. I'm going to visit the rail head."

"You can't"

"I CAN" Phineas surprised himself with the volume. The doctor lowered his eyes.

"You're not ready."

"I will NOT be kept in here." Anger drained him. Slapped his fist on the mattress. "Damn!"

"You've got to avoid exposure. You're not to go out."

"YOU'RE not to give me orders." Brilliant colors. Purples and reds, several shades of yellow, exploded behind Phineas' eyes. The pain beautiful in the way of something that demands your full attention. Phineas sat on the bed. The sound of laughter outside. The realization that an iron rod blasted through his brain and made a hole in his skull. The fear that he was, in some essential way, no longer himself. That something of who he was had leaked out of the hole in his head and left him lacking. Red, yellow star bursts. The sound of iron. Phineas swiped at a chair with his arm. The chair falling. Phineas losing his balance.

Dr. Harlow moved to him, hand reaching down again.

Phineas was learning that explosions could be like music. Each its own symphony of color. Intricate. Elaborate. *Arpeggio* in browns and greens. His arm began to lash out, but he stopped it, grasped the doctor's hand, allowed himself to be pulled up. Dr. Harlow moved to withdraw his hand. Phineas held on. Squeezing. Exerting force.

The doctor jerked his hand away. Flexed the fingers.

Phineas' smile held no warmth.

Oct. 20th. Improving in every respect. Gets out of and into bed with but little assistance; eats and sleeps well. The fungi have disappeared. The opening in the top of the head is closing up rapidly, with a firm membranous tissue.

Faces. Thomas. Henry.

Phineas sat up. Room wobbled. Faces elongated, returned to shape. Heads nodded.

"Phineas." "How you feeling?"

He shrugged. What to say. "Glad you came."

Shuffling feet. The look in their eyes. "Hard to get away. You know."

"We tried to come sooner. You weren't so well for a time there."

"It's okay."

"You're looking good, Phineas." Their eyes betrayed them. Thomas, especially, who could not lie well. Phineas had seen the look – where – in the faces of men who confront death.

"I'm eager to get back."

"Sure, Phineas, but take it slow." "Listen to your doctor."

"To HELL with him" Phineas wiped a hand across his mouth, where spittle had emerged. "To hell with him."

"Even so, Phineas –"

"Are you past Leicester?"

A smile between them. "Up past Cornwall." Henry: "I'm very proud of my men – the men."

Purple. Burgundy. Black.

"We should go." "You need to rest." "We'll come soon, eh?"

Mumbling. "The hell you will."

Yellow. The yellow of spring sunrise.

ANGLE: We began by having one of us photograph Gage's skull, inside and out. The next step was to obtain a skull X-ray as well as a set of precise measurements relative to bone landmarks. Using these detailed photographs and a brain-imaging technique called positron emission tomography, we were able to reconstruct his three-dimensional brain and the focal point of his injuries on a computer. Once the likely trajectory was determined, we could look at affected brain areas and compare to contemporary studies.

Nov. 8th. Fifty-sixth day. Sits up most of the time during the day. Appetite good, though he is not allowed a full diet. Pulse 65. Sleeps well, and says he has not any pain in his head.

Walking. Dizziness. The need to concentrate to keep the ground from moving under him. The smell of earth, of horses and food and life. Leicester Junction, thriving in the railroad's wake, no longer the base camp, the work now more than two miles north, still the town had harnessed the future. Phineas out for a stroll. Eyes on him. Tentative voices.

"Hello, Phineas."

"Good to see you about."

How strangers could know him. How he could shrink inside himself. The look in eyes that won't meet his. In eyes that will.

"You shouldn't have gone out." The room above the tavern. Near sunset. "You don't have the strength."

Sunlight spilled through the window. The pain purple-pink. Phineas focused the light in his eye on his doctor. "Do you think it's possible that something escaped?"

The room's walls an eggshell color. The doctor's hands hovered around Phineas' skull.

"Escaped?" Deft fingers removed bandages. Probed. "There was some tissue loss. Minor. Ultimately insignificant." As the doc-

84

tor spoke these words, he wondered. Wondered about a rod moving through a brain. About the part of the brain the rod passed through. Wondered about Phineas' erratic behavior. About the man his friends described, careful, cautious, steady.

"Was anything else found on the ground? Near the rod?" What does the soul look like, shattered, in the dust.

Dr. Harlow paused, looked at his patient.

"Pieces of me?"

A chill ran along the doctor's arm. Years later, after Phineas' death, Dr. Harlow would think about that moment, in that room, would begin to grasp the real meaning of Phineas' question as he wrote an article speculating on the possibility that there is a locatable moral center in the brain. But what could be gained by planting doubt.

Dr. Harlow chuckled. "Don't worry. You're all here. The road to recovery."

Nov. 18th. Is walking about room again, and appears to be in a way of recovering, if he can be controlled. Has recently had several pieces of bone pass into the fauces, which he expelled from the mouth.

First frost. Fire in the hearth. Inside Phineas' head, a particularly colorful day.

Dr. Harlow on his stool. "Have you thought about it?"

Vermilion. "Hmm?"

"What you're going to do. An office job."

"I couldn't." Butterscotch. "It's being out there, being part of it."

The sound of rail dropping to the ground. The thought of inexorable movement forward.

"You've had severe trauma."

Moisture beaded on the outside of the windows. Veins of frost dissolved.

Dr. Harlow taking notes.

Jade. The impulse to hurt. "It would be so easy."

Dr. Harlow, pen in hand, looking up. "What?"

"An accident." A log popped in the fire. "Waiting for a moment with Henry on a ledge below me, the others out of the way. Easy to say that Henry never heard the 'Stand clear,' that I never saw him." Black. Henry falling. Rock raining down on him. Phineas listened to the words coming out of his mouth. Inside, a scream. A lament.

Dr. Harlow's face was ashen. He didn't know how to respond. How to characterize this behavior. Papers sat idly on his lap.

Phineas gestured at them, a smile, a wince dancing at the edges of his mouth. "Might I see your notes?"

The doctor's eyes refocused on the room. On the patient. "Nothing very interesting," he said. "And the handwriting's impossible."

Dream state. Thrashing on his bed. He saw his deathbed, years hence. Convulsions. Phineas had returned to his mother's house, weary from travel. The colors were no longer beautiful. No longer mesmerizing, though he continued to marvel that so many gradations were possible. Shivering. A glimpse of a boat, a cold stinking boat, carrying him somewhere. He had not planned it this way. Could not keep a job. His mother's words in a letter: "you always find *something* that doesn't suit you." Can't help it. He would wander the world. He would die in his mother's house. He had not planned it this way. Was not this person his words revealed. The colors. The cold. Unfamiliar places. The look in eyes that won't meet his. In eyes that will.

Jan. 1, 1849. The opening in the top of the head entirely closed, and the brain shut out from view, though every pulsation could be distinctly seen and felt. General appearance good; stands erect, with his head inclined slightly towards the right side. The left side of the face is wider than the right side, the left molar bone being more prominent than its fellow. Applied for his situation as foreman, but is undecided whether to work or travel.

ANGLE: Unassisted by the tools of experimental neuropsychology available today, John Harlow came to equate Gage's cognitive and behavioral changes with a presumed area of focal damage in the frontal region. Other cases of neurological damage at that time were confirming the brain's foundation for language, motor function, and perception. Gage's case indicated that perhaps there were structures in the human brain dedicated to the planning and execution of personally and socially suitable behavior, to the aspect of reasoning known as rationality.

I lost all trace of him, and had well nigh abandoned all expectation of ever hearing from him again. As good fortune would have it, however, in July 1866, I was able to learn the address of his mother. From her I learned that Gage was dead.

In August 1852, nearly four years after his injury, he had turned his back upon New England, never to return. He conceived a great fondness for pets and souvenirs, only exceeded by his attachment for his tamping iron, which was his constant companion during the remainder of his life [and which was, in fact, buried with him]. He engaged with a man going to Chile to establish a line of coaches. He moved to San Francisco. Spent time in New York, at Barnum's. Worked for a farmer in Santa Clara. In February 1861, while sitting at dinner, he fell in a fit, and soon after had two or three fits in succession, which led to his death at age 37.

I desire to gratefully express my obligations, and those of the profession, to D.D. Shattuck, Esq., brother-in-law of the deceased; to Dr. Coon, Mayor of San Francisco, and to Dr. J.D.B. Stillman, for their kind cooperation in executing my plans for obtaining the head and tamping iron, and for their fidelity in personally superintending the opening of the grave and forwarding what we so much desired to see.[2]

notes

Italicized portions are paraphrased and/or excerpted from Dr. Harlow's journal or his June 1868 presentation to the Mass. Medical Society. (Pub. Mass. Medical Society, 2, 327 [1868])

[1,2] *John M. Harlow, M.D., in a presentation before the Massachusetts Medical Society, June 3, 1868*

Where Morning Finds You

"ANY SIGN OF HIM? He turn up yet?"

My sister has answered the phone on the fourth ring. I was afraid she wasn't home at all. We had arranged the time that I would call, and I had to search frantically for a pay phone, to gauge my drive time to make it to an offramp, then find a pay phone outside a convenience store, at exactly 2:00 a.m. The desert breeze is still warm.

"No," she says. "Nothing." I can hear Spanish radio playing in the background, the music loud enough to be distracting. I wonder why she doesn't turn it down. I wonder when she began listening to Spanish radio. "Where are you?" she asks.

I look around before I answer, though I already know, by the words on the road sign that led me off of Interstate 15. "Yermo. Outside a Circle K." Inside the store a middle-aged man in an orange smock watches me talk on a pay phone, talk to my only sister about our missing father. "Where have you been looking?"

"Fanning out in expanding circles from the supermarket." My sister was a math whiz in college. Very analytical. I don't know how she ended up a sous chef at a steak house in North Las Vegas. But then there are a lot of things I don't know. "Then expanding circles from home."

Traces of sand graze my skin, carried on the warm air. I don't even ask about the police. I learned years ago, from movies, that they don't consider someone missing until they've been gone at least twenty-four hours. What I do ask her is about the music. Why she doesn't turn it down. That it's so loud now I can't even hear her. I'm on a fucking pay phone, I say. Consider the circumstances.

"There," she says. "I'm in the kitchen now. Is that better?" And it is. The lilt of samba now serves as background to our meandering urgency. "It's usually better in the kitchen. I try to keep walking around to find the spot where it's quietest."

"Why don't you just turn it down?"

"How can I turn it down?"

"You know, the little volume knob on the radio?"

She laughs. "Since when do I listen to Spanish radio? It comes over the phone line. You haven't noticed it before?"

I tell her I haven't. When I call her from my home, I don't notice it. A ballad takes over from the samba. The man in the covenience store still watches me, through his black-rimmed eyeglasses, through the glass of the storefront, through my own glasses, our eyes meet for a moment and I'm reminded of my father.

"I'm going back out there," my sister says. "Call me in two hours."

Interstate 15 carves its way through the southern Mojave Desert, connecting Los Angeles to Las Vegas. Five hours from Santa Monica. I left my house at midnight, right after the call from my sister, telling me that my father, who has lately been subject to occasional spells of disorientation and forgetfulness, had apparantly wandered out of the grocery store where she'd taken him to buy some milk, after they'd had dinner together and before she was going to drive him home. She'd spent a few hours looking for him, first in and around the market, then figuring that he must have gone home, before calling me. My mother, his partner for thirty-eight years, died several months ago. He's been depressed. Frustrated that he can't just pick up the pieces and get on with it. Part of a generation and an Irish heritage that resists emotion. Considers it something to be wrestled into submission. Defeat grief. But life doesn't necessarily cooperate. Forced retirement and the death of a spouse within six months. No wonder he's a little disoriented. Still, it's hard not to think it might be something else. Something even less easily worked through. This isn't like him.

I think of a couple times I've heard him say he doesn't see any point in going on. That there's nothing for him. I don't know what to think. Then I find myself thinking about the last time I was driving frantically in the middle of the night, this same road, this same time, this same knot in the middle of my stomach, after the same kind of phone call from my sister. My father only started using the phone after my mother died. Back then, that last time, my sister called to tell me my mother's heart was failing. That it didn't look like she could last more than a couple of hours. And I hung up the phone and drove, faster than I dared think about, yet feeling like the car was moving through water, no way to shorten the three hundred fourteen miles between myself and the hospital where my mother lay, no way to stop the brain from thinking that I should have gone earlier, should have been there when I first heard there was trouble, when I first heard of the most recent heart attack. That I knew the signs weren't good, that she couldn't keep fighting much longer, that her heart wouldn't take many more of these eruptions. But she had seemed so confident of pulling through. She had sounded determined on the phone. Had said, "Come up when you can. In a couple of weeks. I'll be home then." Had said, "There's no way I'm going to miss the birth of my grandchild."

Deciding this could go on indefinitely, that I could confront this decision several times a year for ever. Wondering is this the time that it's serious, the time I should be there? Deciding I couldn't keep making the drive time after time. That this wasn't likely to be it. That I had factors to consider. Work deadlines. A wife, pregnant with our first child, due in a matter of weeks. The drive interminable yet evaporating so the moment of getting out of the car at the hospital seemed almost concurrent with the phone call.

I didn't make it. Ten minutes, my sister told me. The body lay on the bed behind my sister, hands folded across the stomach, quiet, my father standing over it. Ten minutes ago, my sister told me. Ten minutes ago, she was still here, my sister said. I can't believe it.

So now I'm driving again in the middle of the night, although everything is probably fine, and I've got a knot in my stomach although there's probably nothing to worry about, and I turn on the radio this time to keep my mind from racing, from playing back the eerie similarities. I hit the scan button, and when the scanning stops the speakers play Spanish pop music and I don't change the station.

At 4:00 in the morning, I'm waiting to use a pay phone.

I'm parked in front of the Mohawk Cafe in Nipton, California and I'm a few minutes late because I had to go a ways off the interstate to find a phone. I don't want to try to find another one, so I decide I'll wait it out. The phone is being used by a girl in her late teens, a white sleeveless cotton blouse, blue jeans. Long, dark hair blown around by a still, hot wind. She's arguing with someone on the phone, moving and twisting her body to the minimal extent the short metal phone cord allows. She's trying to convince the person on the other end of something. I'm looking at the facade, a pink stucco with large letters painted in black MOHAWK CAFE, NIPTON, CALIF. POP. 380 and I'm thinking that's a funny thing to put on a sign, but then it's funny that the bar is open at 4:00 a.m. in this desolate town and that I'm waiting to use the pay phone.

The wind blows dust in swirls across the entrance, an aluminum screen door that is the only hole in the front of the building. Behind the cafe, the desert is big. The girl slams the receiver in place and spins into the bar. For a minute, I can't remember my sister's phone number. I never write them down. I have an amazing capacity for remembering them. It's a gift, I tell people.

"You're late," she says, accompanied by what I think is the voice of Linda Ronstadt doing a song from her Mexican album.

"Had to wait for a phone," I say.

"Where are you?"

"Mohawk Cafe. Nipton, California. Population 380."

"You're a strange person," she says. The probable Linda Ronstadt fades out, replaced by a mariachi tune.

"Well?"

"Nothing," she says. "*Nada*."

"What next?"

"I don't know. I'm running out of ideas." Music fills the silence. It's like being on hold and having a conversation, all at once. "Do you think he's okay? I mean, this isn't like him."

I think for a minute, mostly about how honest I want to be.

"No," I say. "I don't think he's okay. But he needs to decide to get on with his life. We can't do that for him." Suddenly I feel like Dr. Phil.

"I mean now. Tonight. Do you think he's alright?"

"I don't know. I don't want to think about it. I just want to get there." We're an east coast family. We're a little uncomfortable in the desert. We prefer smaller spaces.

"How much longer?"

"Less than two hours." This has become the standard unit of measuring time. "You going back out?"

"Yeah. I'm going to try the parks. He sometimes likes to walk in the evenings." She must not be in the kitchen. The music has gotten louder. She has an antique stove in her kitchen, given to her by a man she lived with for eight years, a man she kicked out last year, right before my mom died, a man who very much wants to get back together. She's not sure what she wants. She says right now it's a matter of choosing not to run. Of waking up each day and choosing not to run. Learning to live with an empty place inside.

"You're not in the kitchen, are you?"

She laughs. "It's been like this for a few weeks. Driving me crazy."

"Have you called the phone company?"

"They insist it's not the line. That it's not their problem."

"So where's it coming from?"

"That's what I said. They said that's not for them to figure out. They said there was a part I could get at Radio Shack. The guy at Radio Shack said he'd sell it to me, but it wouldn't fix the problem. He said it was a question of hounding the phone company into submission."

Something about that makes me feel sad, as though all our efforts are merely distractions to take our attention away from the fact that people vanish every day. People die. "Maybe it's something you could get used to," I say, in a hurry again. "I'll see you soon."

The last time I saw my father we had one of our rare conversations. I had been offered a full-time job writing advertising copy, and I was trying to decide between the security of that offer and the freedom of the freelance life. His first reaction was to get mad. He said where did I get off complaining about a choice of well-paying jobs when he couldn't even find part-time work. We were sitting in a coffee shop. Dark wood beams ran above the counter, the vinyl of the booths was a rich burgundy and his voice was loud enough to make me a little uncomfortable. I could see his point, but still. This is my life, I said. What do you want me to do about that? His face softened a little.

"I wouldn't want to be young today," he told me then. "We didn't have so many choices -- at least I didn't -- but we knew where we fit. Who we were." His voice trailed off. I remember thinking at that moment how ironic it all was. For years, I'd tried to get my dad to talk, to open up a little, and now that he was, it made me uncomfortable. Part of me wished he'd stop. I find now, with a child of my own, that I can't blame him as I'd like to for the distance that's separated us all these years. For the silence. I have my own limitations.

After less than a year, I have difficulty remembering things about my mother. I remember vague, general things -- she was small and she didn't have much hair and she was a child in so many ways but I don't remember moments. Incidents. I sometimes focus on her face, just to hold it in my memory, to make sure I don't lose it. And I practice remembering moments, reconstructing pieces of her life, of our lives together. I practice with other people, too. As a hedge against loss. I concentrate on picturing my father's face. My wife's. My child's.

Reaching Las Vegas in the dim, early morning is disorienting. Driving for hours through desert, in darkness, in quiet, with only the illumination of your own headlights. Then lights flickering in the distance, the twinkling of a little community that might be a mirage. Then you're in the midst of it, dizzying, driving through neon, bulbs flashing, beckoning. The eyes don't focus. They try to shut out all the activity. Sensory overload.

It's six a.m. and I can't find my sister's house. She gives lousy directions. We communicate very differently, she and I. I can't tell if I'm in the right neighborhood, or on the wrong side of town.

I am not ready for my father to die, because I cannot, still, picture his face when I close my eyes, or conjure the sound of his voice. I keep hoping to see him by the side of the road. To turn a corner and see him walking along, watching the sun rise. I imagine that I will stop at a pay phone outside a Circle K and I will call my sister, and the man in the orange smock who works at the store will watch me through the window, and the Spanish music will make it hard to hear, and my sister will answer the phone.

He's here, she'll say. He's alright. Do you want to talk to him?

And she'll put him on the phone, and there'll be sheepish hellos and then he'll tell me that he went to a hotel bar and got a little drunk, then sat on a bench at the park and talked to himself about his life. It's time to get on with it, he'll say, then he'll pause a little and he'll say, I miss her. Then, after a minute, my sister will get back on the phone and I'll joke with her about her bad directions, and then she'll get me there, in time for breakfast.

Figure With Meat

fig. 1.1 (uncooked)

Poor Otto in the infinite desert.

"Don't come to me this broken puppy dog," says Horst. Pie-faced Horst. Heavyweight picture of eternal youth. Short, sandy hair. Pale pink flesh. Parked in a leather armchair in a dark corner of his posh parlor. "You disdained Floriana from the beginning. It's a mystery what she saw in you."

Spring sunlight illumines gaunt, nail-biting Otto. What can he say? Floriana. Perpetual hair. Endless flowing ego. Despite himself, he can't shake her. "I don't want to talk about Floriana."

Dark wood. Rich leather. A regatta sun through tall draped windows. "What, then?" demands Horst.

But Otto cannot get to it so quickly or directly. It is not unusual for Otto to forget why he came. Otto struggles to make eye contact. Otto is here to talk about purity. To wring his hands before his old friend and seek sympathy. Instead, peevish: "She won't sleep with you. You reek."

Horst hugs a slab of raw meat to his chest. Slaughterhouse-sized. A vein runs through the rich red face of it. A second slab propped in the leather chair beside him like a talk show guest. "Floriana is turned on by hostility. If you'd seen that, she'd still be with you." A leathery layer of ecru fat under Horst's hand. He's practicing poses. His new discovery a portraitist. A graduate of graphic novels. "She's trying to have the painting stopped. People for the Ethical Treatment of Raw Meat, or some such."

"Her art is insipid." Otto paces. Prematurely gray.

Horst smiles. "You overlooked that when she was fucking you." Otto starts to speak, but Horst cuts him off with a wave. "She's a woman of her time. She knows how to speak to the public." The room carries the faint odor of aging meat. Horst shifts in his chair without losing his grip on the beef. His fingers discolored, vaguely burgundy. "I'm glad she hurt you." He slaps the slab. "Perhaps it will toughen you up."

The words sting. Otto stands on a carpet crafted from some sort of animal fur. He is a painter whose talent easily draws interest from galleries – interest that tends to fade when they see the fullness of his work. He stares at his feet. "They're not going to do the show," he says.

"What are we talking about?"

"Christ in the Wilderness," Otto says. A series of abstract oils based on Jesus' bedeviled desert days. "Kroner Gallery. They passed."

"Of course they passed. Abstractions on temptation and suffering. How much would you have people endure?"

On the wall, a framed newspaper photograph of alligator races, Horst presiding proudly over a roomful of revelers. Everything Horst touches finds favor. Otto looks away. "They called it *stubbornly difficult.*"

Horst's laugh echoes around the room. "Perfect," he says. "True."

Otto sulks in Horst's sunlight. "I'm not sure how much more I have in me."

"Good. How old are you Otto? Are you nineteen? Do you suffer for your art? No one cares. People make paintings. They sell them." Horst's face turns a slow, comfortable crimson. It's impossible to tell if it's a reflection from the beef, or him warming to his subject. "Let me tell you something. A pair of pigs from a commercial have been moved into luxury retirement quarters in the next block. They flew on television, so now they'll never become bacon. And you. You can't pay your bills. Their concierge would not receive you. You have to face facts."

Otto takes a series of quick, short breaths. Opens his arms in a gesture that encompasses Horst, the sides of beef, the parlor. He squints into sunlight. "This is not art. You're recreating a 1950s Francis Bacon painting."

Horst's face contracts, a sour pickle scowl. "How many people know that painting? Besides, the reference – the humor – makes it work," says Horst. "Bacon. Meat. All the compelling work today is done by carnivores." Horst's scowl segues to a smile. He cocks his head subtly. "The painting has already sold, Otto. Based on a sketch and a bio. This is my skill. Should I apologize?" He pats the meat. "I could describe this to any Jew at the supermarket, hug a roast beef to my chest and double the market price. I could sell and re-sell the idea and live well for five years without ever having the painting done. Think about that Otto. Why are you here Otto?"

Otto strains to remember. Can't. "Keeping tabs on the devil."

A belly laugh. "Bless you." Horst blows him a kiss. "And who are you?"

"The voice in the wilderness. Witness to temptation."

"Christ," says Horst. "Snake charm. Paltry promises. *Bread.* Who couldn't say no. Think if your Christ had been offered steak. Not hypothetical bread, but flesh and blood meat, dripping in front of him. I question whether his response had been so noble, would it have survived the centuries if he'd been offered meat."

fig. 1.2 (how they met)
Up Your Alley – bowling lanes, bar and grill. An art opening on a frigid February night. Festive crowd. Finger foods. Flash bulbs. Paintings adorn three walls. A DJ spins dance tunes, the lanes deco-

rated as if for a county fair, lined with streamers in green and gold. A Horstian extravaganza-in-the-making.

Otto, in black mock turtleneck and jeans, sips red wine from a plastic cup and suffers. Horst's latest discovery a flame-haired hipster from the heartland with this series of acrylics: boys – brothers – at play with pet alligators. The reptiles distorted. Their alligatorness exaggerated. Vaguely sexualized. No sign yet of the boy artist, or his handler. Otto, making the effort to not appear haughty, hangs at the periphery. The crowd in clusters, the usual people in the usual conversations. The room's edges fuzzy in Otto's vision – too much wine? Otto sees a stunning woman in a shiny dress. She's new. The dress, festooned with a giant bow in the back, the same color –the same fabric – as the streamers. Otto suspects the hand of Horst: a hired hottie. Nonetheless, he's on his way to ask her about color coordination when he hears a voice in his ear.

"It's Waldo, isn't it?" A woman stands before him. Long face, high cheekbones, flowing burgundy scarf tied loosely about her neck. A dancer's body. A chignon of thick silver hair. A shade that somehow Otto has never seen.

"Otto," he says.

"Of course." Long fingers touch his arm. "I'm Floriana." An air of casual sexuality. Otto takes it in. "Horst insisted we meet. Otto will amuse you, he promised. But I'm bad with names. I've been asking everyone, 'Where's Waldo? Where's Waldo?'"

Otto finds himself captivated by the knot of hair. Silver, not gray. There's a lushness. A purity. And Otto nearly a year without a woman.

A reporter from the *Globe*, a young woman Otto recognizes as the paper's second-string art critic, hovers within striking distance. Blunt-cut, high-gloss black hair. Long legs. Messenger bag slung across her shoulders. Some nights the whole world is seductive. Floriana stands close beside him, regarding a painting of a boy holding a dwarf alligator aloft for his young brother's appreciation.

"What do you think?" Floriana asks. She wears a thin cotton dress. She touches his arm so softly he shivers.

"Skilled," says Otto. "Still, flat. I long for texture. Accumulating paint. Something to arouse desire." Otto aware of her closeness – the delicate hair of her arm touching his. "You?"

The *Globe* reporter starts toward them. Otto puts his back between her and Floriana. "Like you," Floriana says, "I admire the skill."

Voices behind them. One he recognizes. Alice, a young artist whose last project involved coordinating the lights in a dormitory – on, off, on – into simple geometric patterns, has intercepted the *Globe* reporter. "My next project will be more conceptual," she says. "M&M candies grouped by color."

"Really?" The reporter's voice. "Interesting."

Otto hates this. Give him a spirits-soaked rag and paint under his nails. A solo spotlight where he can beat his breast. He focuses on Floriana's delicate ear. The silver strands tucked behind. He bulges. Feels his face flush.

"Horst tells me you make paintings of sand," she says.

Otto flushes. "Meditations on temptation and desire. Studies in virtue."

She nods vaguely.

Otto remembers now hearing her name around town. A New York transplant. Horst represents her. Delicate watercolors and ink. Facile work that sells well. A rumor she's an ex-nun. Otto finds this inexplicably sexy. He wants to dismiss her but can't. Instead, he imagines her cloistered. Feels a stirring in his pants. "Didn't Horst tell me you work with animals?"

She tosses her head. A stray strand of hair crosses her forehead. "Have you ever experienced monkeys in the wild?"

"Come again?" Otto leans forward, hungry. He can scarcely focus.

"Monkeys," she says. "The squirrel monkey is endangered in Bolivia, Peru, Paraguay." Floriana's head moves slightly as she speaks. Her cheeks red, inflamed.

"Fascinating," Otto says. "Tell me more."

"There's an intelligence," she says. "A dignity. I find myself drawn to animal advocacy, more and more."

"But your art?"

"Where to focus one's energy," she says. "It's always the question. My art is respite. Relaxation."

Otto tastes acid. He works to keep his face impassive. Despite disgust, his erection grows.

Then, a trumpet fanfare. A buzz of voices. They turn to witness a parting of the crowd. Horst in waistcoat, green and gold, arm linked with the flame-haired boy wonder. Behind them, a procession set to a throbbing dance beat. The crowd claps to the rhythm. A series of alligators, wearing silk sashes with names and numbers, each accompanied by a handler in waistcoat and color-coded cummerbund. Laughter. Applause. Otto blanches. Floriana drifts closer to the action, toward the lanes where the reptiles prepare to race.

Horst beams. Greets the throngs. "Laaadies and gentlemen." His best race-track announcer voice. "Welcome one and all. Here are the entrants in tonight's feature race." From somewhere, a drum roll. The artist engrossed in conversation, surrounded. All others engulfed in Horst, who straddles the center lanes. Behind him, by the pin setters, gators and their grooms at the starting gate. "In lane one," Horst announces, "sporting a gold silk sash…" He introduces each gator. Wendell. Wally. Warren. Wilfred. Waldo.

Betting sheets emerge and are collected by Horst minions. Otto stands frozen. Voices, music echo as if in a dream. The voice at his ear pulls him back.

"Well?" Beside him, Horst beams.

Otto's mouth dry. "You've outdone yourself."

"Thank you."

"It's obscene."

Horst puts an arm around Otto, his smile undimmed. "Twenty bucks says I'll have fucked Floriana by the end of February."

A reporter grabs Horst's arm and he's gone. His head minion announces one minute to post time. Then Floriana is beside Otto again. She hands him a slip of paper. "I've bet on Waldo, for you."

Otto grunts. The room fades. His sightline fixes on Floriana. Scorn fuels his nascent passion. His bulge belies his beliefs. He licks his lips: "You repulse me, in a way I find irresistible."

fig. 1.3 (shadow)

"The world is fading, Horst."

"Blah blah blah the end of history blah blah blah. Tedious postmodernism. Assemblages. A little Horstian wisdom: live today, breathe the air, fuck the women. Make paintings if you must, but Christ, Otto, get over yourself. Look around you. What do you see?"

Otto sees water, the reservoir, gentle hills thick with pine. You'd never know you were within a hundred yards of a highway.

"Oasis," says Otto.

"Wrong." Horst stabs a finger in the air. "Opportunity." He gestures across the water. His eyes behind the sleek sunglasses athletes wear. "What would you say if I told you that yesterday I signed onto a development deal – townhouses and artists' lofts. A little left bank theme park starting at 750k. What would you say to that."

Otto says nothing. What can Otto say that will not make Horst laugh.

A mockingbird calls.

Even in the open air Horst smells vaguely of raw meat. "You know, if you could pull your head out of your ass for five minutes, I'd hire you to manage my affairs."

"I mean literally, Horst. My vision. It's hereditary." Birch trees. Buds verge on blossom. "An unusual form of optic neuropathy. The loss of central sight, yes, but more. The slow fade of color. The encroachment of shadow."

Horst, leather-gloved hands at his side, surveys the area. The distant whoosh of highway traffic. "The *fuck* are you talking about?"

"I'm losing my vision."

"See an optometrist. Get glasses."

"In two years, I could be legally blind."

"In two days, we could both be dead. Is this a diagnosis? Have you seen a doctor?"

"You know how I feel about doctors." They have history together. Otto knows that Horst is Harold from Englewood, who changed his name and provenance for art school. "I know what's happening, Horst. I had an uncle…"

"You're a piece of work. A mediocre painter loses his sight. How romantic. How convenient if it were true." Residual chill in the air. "What are you working on?"

"Are you listening? I'm losing my sight."

"Last year it was Parkinson's. You had an estranged half-sister." Horst squeezes his gloved hands into fists. "You can't paint, can you?"

Otto, shamed, shakes his head.

"You're sulking because the gallery didn't like your sand paintings. Wake up, Otto. Buy property. Cut down trees. Save the fucking reptiles."

Did Otto believe he would find a sympathetic ear? Truth is, he's terrified of the blank canvas. Always has been. Now more than ever, what will he paint, and why?

"By the way," Horst says, "did I introduce you to my boots?" He points to each foot in turn. "You remember Wilfred," he says. "Waldo."

Otto feels his face pinch.

Horst beside him. "*Kidding*. You are so goddamned earnest. It will lead to erectile dysfunction, if it hasn't already."

Otto lost in the romance of his own imagined demise. Objects on the periphery less focused than last week. Less true. The birch silhouetted. The carpet of pine needles camel-colored. Shouldn't they be more vibrant, coppery? "What if this is the end?"

Horst has shifted his gaze. Head and torso in slow panorama. Surveying possibilities. Converting land to cash.

"Let me tell you a story, Otto." It is as if Horst is dictating into a tape machine. As if Otto is not there. "A man in my building, Slovak, he's in the hospital. Tried to kill himself." Horst pauses for effect. "He'd been creative with his taxes, but not clever. IRS catching up, he's afraid he'll lose everything. Decides to off himself." They stare at the reservoir, the woods beyond. In two years, what will Otto see here? "He sticks his head in a homemade guillotine. Homemade fucking guillotine. Botches the job. Of course, he'll live. Do you see my point, Otto?"

Otto sees March wind stirring pine boughs. Otto has always looked older and felt younger than he is.

"This is the future I see for you, Otto. Some cockeyed romantic demise and you'll fuck it up."

fig. 1.4 (rust)

Otto and Floriana. A late-night walk. Misted moon just past full. Main Street. Soft shadows, shops and restaurants. Dimly reflected silhouettes. The river, where within weeks the boat tour season will begin. Before he dies, Otto determines, he will go on a booze cruise with Floriana. First, certain things to address. A hint of rusted steel in the air as they approach the old bridge.

"You can make more substantive art, Floriana." A black lacquered chopstick holds her hair behind her head. Otto does not tire of touching it. "Watercolor is frivolous. Make a shift. Get serious."

He wraps an arm around her. Pulls her close. Historically he has done well with women, for periods of weeks.

She pulls away. Gives him a look that says, *I've been reviewed in the New York Times.* "What is art, Otto? Narcissism. I can't look past what needs to be accomplished in the world. Be of service."

"No," Otto insists. "Artistic vision, faithfully cultivated. We're prophets."

"Naïve, Otto. Endearing at 25. Tedious at 45."

"John the Baptist," Otto says. "Moses in the wilderness."

"Please, Otto. I have no patience."

"But the nunnery?"

"Two years of Catholic school. An exaggeration. An air of mystery on a bio." Her breasts roam free under a thin dress. Her coat open. "Goodbye, Otto. Introspection leaves you flaccid. I want jousting. A lance."

"It's been a month. I'll evolve. Stiffen."

"We live in a postmodern age. Time accelerates. The past is dead."

And that was that.

Otto recalls this moment weeks later, walking alone across the same steel bridge in an unforgiving April wind. He cannot bring the moment, the evening, his life into focus. He has taken to squinting, as if that will increase acuity. His field of vision *has* faded some. He feels his age. The rush of a river waterfall to his right. The glint of streetlights in the water. Ahead, by the railroad tracks, a fat man in a wool Cossack's coat, a pair of pink leashes attached to waddling pets. Are the pets pink? Does he see curly tails? Otto blinks and stares, but can't discern. Which would be worse: to lose vision, or to view the world through Horst eyes? Otto looks at the river. Smells sulfur. Lifts his eyes to the street. Leashes lead the Cossack's coat around the corner, out of sight. At home, Otto will reconstruct: what does Otto see (experience) and what (world) does he create for himself, in the shadows.

fig. 1.5 (featherless)

Otto in the world of men.

Horst moves briskly beside him in the early evening. Clutches a paper coffee cup. Long strides along the cinder path behind Town Hall, where white Christmas lights in stunted beech trees twinkle in mid-May. It seems to Otto that, despite spring, darkness is forever descending. He is painting, but tentatively. Joylessly. He finds the background of a new canvas going red-black. Intense darkness that attracts the eye, swallows vision. Bells in the clock tower chime seven. Horst in mid-monologue.

"She's traveling. Involved. Photo ops. London. India. I get headlines – ailing bluefish saved by homemade life jacket. Elephants used to demolish illegally built houses in Benares." They moved to this former mill town for the novelty. Now they blame each other, and secretly revisit the city for their favorite restaurants. "And her beloved monkeys. Pawns in a political game. Global economy versus biosphere. This is what I get, Otto. Tabloid headlines. Stories instead of sex."

Otto half-listening. Pondering a question his Jesuit therapist had asked him, weeks back: *which are you, Jesus or John the Baptist?* Otto broods. He is the voice in the wilderness. But if the Baptist, who or what is the Christ to which he points? What coming does he foretell? If these were Horst's preoccupations, Horst would display himself in flowing robes, subsist on locusts and wild honey. Horst would have an answer.

"And all this meat," Horst says. "It's tiresome. Someone should study the psychological impact of prolonged exposure to rotting beef. I admit, much of the charm was the idea of Floriana's reaction. The anger. The acrobatic sex. Without her, it's just so much rancid meat in the hands of a tepid painter. He lacks your skill, Otto. There, I said it. Plus, it's costly. I have prospects that need my attention. Which reminds me. I want you to do something for me. I'll pay you. Make a house call on the pigs. Present your card to Gaspar, the concierge. See will they receive you. I want to commission a portrait – pigs in retirement. Don't say no. It's for your edification. You think you're better than everyone. It's one reason people don't like you."

Otto finds it impossible to tell when Horst is serious. What is speculative and what is real. "Pigs," he says.

Horst a belly laugh. "A small matter, Otto. A temporary zoning variance. Do this for me. For you. I need to reach Floriana. I need to know her stance on the pigs. Where is she on luxury retirement units for pork. Meanwhile, Otto, I have projects. A man approached me, a geneticist or so he says. Wants to increase the poultry populations in warm climates. Claims to have developed a featherless chicken. I'm intrigued."

fig. 1.6 (miserere)

Otto paints at Horst's place. Gorecki's saddest music behind him. Horst on the road, following Floriana – deeply smitten, despite himself. Otto earns extra cash house-sitting. Dawn Upshaw's voice rises above cellos, violas. Otto daubed in late afternoon sun. A trio of pages hang from a wire atop his easel. He works from old watercolors. Child's bible images. Christ crowned in thorns. Moses wandering. Paint what you see. What does Otto see? How to express that no matter the cause, the light is fading. There is no doctor for this.

Otto has met Gaspar, the concierge in the neighboring building. Gaspar denies the existence of the pigs. Overcoming his personal horror, determined to validate his vision, Otto wears dark glasses, adopts a pre-WWII espionage air. With a firm grip on his arm, Gaspar shunts Otto into a corner, and in an urgent whisper demands, "What pigs? Who sent you?"

Gaspar a gulag survivor from the former Soviet Union, an Uzbeki émigré who shuts down talk of the past. But Otto doesn't know this so Otto persists: "Everyone knows."

A glare from Gaspar speaks of darknesses Otto cannot imagine. Gaspar's face, inches away. A sardine smell. "What do you fear most?" he hisses. Otto wavers. His knees knock. Whatever fear Gaspar felt fades. "Get out of my building before I bite your leg, little man."

Otto returns days later, with a broiled chicken and a bottle of house red. Lobby visits lead to lengthy conversations. Over time, Gaspar does not deny the existence of the pigs. But does not acknowledge. Will not provide introductions.

Now, brushes beside Otto in a jar. His fingers tell the story of that day's work in reds, browns, blacks. He tastes linseed oil as he nibbles his nails. The canvas began as sand and sky, ochre and azure. Layers of paint. A topography of textures. Otto alone in a room as the sun fades, Otto squeezing paint from a tube, color and heft on canvas to capture something he cannot put words to. Floriana accomplishes things. Makes impact. An injunction stopped Horst's alligator races. The judge has become a partner in the housing development project. Otto paints. The colors grow darker. Thicken.

fig. 1.7 (pigs in retirement)

"Clever, Otto. Very clever." Horst beaming. Cobalt blue shirt, red ascot, raw rump roast tucked like a football under one arm. "The three-dimensionality. The nod to meat. Compelling. Contemporary. I didn't think you had it in you."

Argyle Skirt Gallery, a cool August night. Cosmos and cranberry martinis. All the drinks this season are pale red and pink. There is a healthy turnout. More, of course, than Otto had expected. The whole event surreal. Dimly lit. If Otto's eyes do not deceive him, two women dressed as Colonial soldiers play foosball in a distant corner. Why are they all here? Otto has done a series of paintings – assemblages – each one a tiny plastic pig glued onto a dark, abstract background. Blood red, brown, black. Otto marvels at the blur of bodies. The work embraced. Otto, wary, wonders why. Themes he has long wrestled with contained finally on canvas? Groanings too deep for words? Or this: he has glued plastic pigs to failed paintings. People smile. Otto, tortured, tries to understand.

Now Floriana, standing next to him. Floral scarf. "Are you happy, Otto? Do your pigs give you pleasure?" He cannot gauge her sincerity.

"Welcome home," he grunts. They stand side by side, evaluating the crowd as if a painting. A press of people. Otto squints to see his pigs at the party's periphery. "What species are you saving now?"

"Be that way," she says. "Do you have any idea the number of birds dead from avian flu the last 10 years? The number of humans? And your friend, with his unroasted beef." Arms folded beside him. She regards his paintings. "I like them," she says. "They're festive." And floats away. Otto would have hope if he did not know from Horst, vivid details of furious sex.

Horst works the room. Otto overhears him spinning a story about a device that can convert a dog's emotional states into language. A crowd, captivated, Horst always at its center, those around him fuzzy. "Bow-lingual," Horst says.

Nine paintings. Nine tiny plastic pigs. A gift from Gaspar. Otto had discovered them aligned on his bathroom sill, basking in late afternoon light. It was two days before he'd had the courage to touch them, to gauge their material reality. Concierge and caretaker, Gaspar waves from amid a knot of young women, red hair, mini-skirts, boots. Otto raises a rose-colored beverage in toast. Paintings begun in desperation, reflections on an increasingly shadowed world. Paintings that had become increasingly abstract. Otto had wallowed, almost happy. Until a day – inevitably – Horst came by to see. "Maybe I was wrong," Horst had said. "Maybe you are losing your sight." Otto had escaped to the bathroom to regroup. Nestled chin on sill. Near his pigs.

Now Horst, *sotto voce.* Conspiratorial. "A trace of humor, Otto. Don't let it get around. You might end up with a career." The same smirk Floriana's face had worn. As if they were in on a joke.

The woman from the *Globe*, with a notebook. Long legs under a black skirt. Mop of raven-black hair. Lively eyes. Head cocked thoughtfully before Pig #5 (Prophet).

"Then where would you be, you and your disdainful pout?" Horst with a death grip on the meat. He has taken to carrying raw garlic in his pockets to combat the smell. Horst winks in the reporter's direction, receives a mischievous smile. Otto blanches – is there nothing Horst doesn't get his fingers on first? "Don't worry," Horst says. "You're safe. Sullen. Fundamentally unlikable." Horst wraps his free arm around Otto's shoulder and squeezes. Otto feels loved, like a side of beef. "But you may yet have a future free from self-inflicted wounds."

They watch Floriana approach the woman from the *Globe*, making notes at Pig #6 (Electric Fence), Otto's favorite. Floriana: "Isn't this delicious?" Reporter: "I like." Otto strains to hear the rest of her response. He catches the words "playful" and "tortured innocence." He turns to Horst for a reading – sarcasm or sincerity – but Horst's head is filled with Floriana.

"Chickens, Otto." A sadness in his voice. "We are at a crossroads. Pray for us. There is absolutely nothing sexy about chickens."

The women have moved on. Otto watches people peruse his art.

"All this is yours." Horst a wide grin that says, *you've given the world amusement.*

Otto's stomach rumbles.

"Christ," Horst says. "You look consumptive. Enjoy tonight. Be miserable tomorrow."

Would it be a crime to sell a painting or two? A taste of recognition in tribute to fading vision. He's stirred by the attention. The buzz. He stays near the middle of the room, to take it in. Ponders ways to punish himself later. "Pleasure is a piece of the human experience," Otto argues. "Authentic."

"Fine," says Horst. "Whatever." Eyes scanning the room. Gaspar has found the Colonial soldiers. Floriana flits by in the foreground. "She colors her hair, Otto. Which I find fantastic. Why anyone would choose gray." And Horst glides away, beef cradled under his arm, trailing a red-haired young mini-skirt.

A figure skirts the edge of Otto's vision. The reporter, back again in front of Pig #5. A stance at once engaged and aloof. There is much to ponder, but Otto can ponder tomorrow. Drawing on deep reserves, he pushes aside angst, narrows his gaze to this woman. Lingers on her legs. Her stark black profile. Her intensity of focus. Her smile. What does she see? She looks over. Catches his eye. Her smile widens. A hint of wickedness. Otto trusts his eyes and moves toward her, through the crowd.

Between the Bar and the Telephone Booth

I'm having a pint of Newcastle, making two stacks of quarters and counting to four hundred-twenty before I call Brendan again.

The phone is down a narrow hall, past the service end of the bar, past the rest rooms. It's in a booth, the old-fashioned kind with a wood frame and a door that squeaks when you close it. The phone still says 25¢ even though it costs 50 to make a call. And it has a little wooden seat that is beginning to be worn to the curve of my ass.

Robert says there's a path worn into the wood from my walking. He says it with a smile, but I think, *fuck, is that who I am.*

All you need to know about the bar is they have Newcastle on tap, and Robert, the day man, is my friend. He plays a lot of Thelonious Monk on the stereo. Robert is a good man.

Thelonious Monk was a good man. There's an apocryphal story about how Monk lost his recording contract, lost his club card – no one wanted to hear his music. So he holed up in his apartment for nine years working to make the music pure enough – so completely itself that maybe people could begin to hear it.

Robert is playing Monk right now. The tune is "Don't Blame Me," and it's lush and jagged and completely itself.

No, I don't have a cell phone. I used to, but I smashed it with a ball peen hammer.

It's just Robert and me in the bar right now. Three, three-thirty. A respectable hour for having a pint. I could be someone who knocked off work early, a special occasion, to meet a friend. Or take in a Red Sox game.

The bar is called Bukowski's, which is unfortunate, and it's populated in the evenings by young men – late twenties, early thirties. You wouldn't believe all the goatees. Excuse me, Van Dykes. Most of these guys are in advertising and already lost.

I come here because of Robert. I followed him here from The Pour House, where he used to work. Don't get the wrong idea. I come here twice a week. Three times, max. I'm making some adjustments in my life, and right now I'm trying to track down the photographer who said he was hired to take pictures of murder victims. Hired by the murderers.

That's right, this photographer told me about some kids in the projects – Bromley-Heath, Cathedral – who've been shooting each other. One group of them hires him – a professional, a photo-journalist – to document the fallen bodies of the other group.

He doesn't know these kids. They call him on his cell phone, tell him a location – *white house, corner of Day and Minden, sidewalk* – and he goes there, finds the body, takes pictures. Six, seven times this has happened. He's there and gone before the police. The body fresh. Three days later, an envelope of cash through his mail slot. Thousand bucks a pop.

"You know what they say," he told me. Sat down the bar from Brendan and I. "One picture is worth a thousand bucks."

I had been making phone calls that day, too. Different situation. That day I was trying to reach Ramona, in town for a couple days after a mini-tour of the Carolinas. Ramona is a Buddhist and a musician with notoriously tragic taste in men. She was going back on the road, and I wanted to see if she was free so I could decide if I was working the next day. But no Ramona. Not at home. Not on her cell.

Robert was playing Monk ("Straight, No Chaser") and laughing at me for the line I was wearing in the floor, but I didn't care. I've learned over the years how to manage my time. I could do seminars. And right then, I needed to reach Ramona. Which made me a captive audience, but also a little distracted when this guy sat down and started talking about the Pro Bowlers Tour.

Plus, Brendan was there, waiting to meet the Dog Lady, who owed him money. Until recently, I didn't realize there was this whole subculture of people waiting to meet people.

But the bowling thing was just a way for the guy to strike up a conversation, a way of saying, *see, I'm not one of those assholes from the ad agency.* "Seriously. You remember them? Dick Weber, Earl Anthony? Fuck, those guys could bowl. I used to go to tournaments. I'd follow them through the Northeast. New York. Jersey. Boring as shit, I know, but there was something about it." He was mid-fifties, little paunch but not bad, you could tell he'd been an athlete. Ruddy skin. Thick coppery hair.

I liked the idea of him.

"You'd watch a guy put together a run," he said. "Weber, the way the ball would hang, flirt with the gutter, then turn, perfect, and he knew it, and after a while you did, too. You could feel the change in the air when somebody had it dialed in."

I looked at Brendan. Brendan looked at me. Brendan's got this Jack Nicholson package – the hairline, the devilish grin, the raised eyebrow half-sneer-sideways-curious-look. We had to decide whether to let this guy in. I rearranged coins on the bar. I wanted Brendan to say. But Brendan just opened and closed the lid on his Marlboro box, so I said, "What do you do?" to the guy.

And he said, "I'm a photographer."

And Brendan, following my lead, asked "what do you take pictures of?"

And the guy said, *lately, mostly dead people.* Then told us his story.

Another thing about Monk: he liked to play blue notes – the ones that live in the space between two keys. He'd work to refine those, to cultivate their rare beauty, believing they were escape hatches from pain. Little pockets of loveliness that could rise up out of the compromises and disappointments of daily life. Sustenance. In my current career, I'm a landscaper. Business is booming, so I can take time here and there, let my employer know when I will and won't be available. I always show up when I say I will, which is more than I can say for some.

I've also been a carpenter, real estate appraiser, building inspector and, for a brief time, manager of a friend's music store. Once, I had career aspirations. Worked at MassPIRG after college. I was young. A crusader. I met my ex-wife there. Life and work intertwined, with purpose and direction. Over time I noticed a difference between me and my colleagues. How it mattered to them in ways it didn't to me. I shifted gears, worked as a staffer for a state senator, and lost myself in that for a few years before it became clear it was just an attempt to hold my soon-to-be-ex's interest. After the divorce, I thought I'd do the landscaper thing for a year or two, until I found myself. Now it's ten, and all I've found is I'm not driven toward much.

What do you do. Guy walks into a bar, tells you a story like that. I couldn't get it out of my head. How he gets into the situation. What crazy way it gives his life shape. I wanted to ask him questions, see if he was for real. But I couldn't find him. Hadn't gotten his name. Today I've got a lead.

"You know that guy?" I ask Robert, who has tuned the TV in to the Sox.

"Which guy?" Manny at the plate, Sox down 2-1 in the fifth.

"Pro Bowlers Tour. Was in the other day. Brendan and I."

Robert shakes his head. "Never seen him before."

Great.

Brendan is interested in this photographer, too, but he's got other priorities. He needs to track down the Dog Lady. Can't make rent if he doesn't. She hired him to paint her bulldog. Portraits. The deal was he would do six, she would buy two. She paid for one in advance. Now, four months later he's finished, the first payment long spent, and he can't get hold of her. She never showed up that day he was waiting, now she doesn't answer her phone.

"I swear to God I never do another commission," he told me.

"That's what you said last time," I reminded him. "The chihuahua incident."

Makes me wonder how people end up doing the things they do. Brendan, who's a fine painter – solo shows in Boston, Brooklyn, Seattle – does these portraits of people's dogs. It's not like he advertises; people find him.

Manny hits a home run with Pedroia on first. Sox up, 3-2. It's May, and they're a half-game ahead of the Yankees. There's hope. Robert wipes glasses and watches the TV.

"Where'd he hit it?" I ask Robert.

"Huh?"

"Where'd he hit it?"

But Robert's eyes don't leave the screen.

I'm forty-two years old, veteran of one marriage, two careers and three midlife crises (to date). I'm known among my friends as a listener more than a talker, and it has occurred to me that this is because no one finds my stories interesting. People don't remember meeting me. But one of the things I'm working on is being so completely myself that people will begin to hear me.

Few weeks ago, I found this book at a used book place: *Everyday Zen.* Started carrying it with me, reading a little here and there. Some days it feels like an answer ("The spirit of questioning is the core practice"), other days like a joke.

I take two quarters from my stacks on the bar and try Brendan again. I've forgotten to count, but it's been way more than four hundred twenty. I'm trying to get him down here. There was another killing last night, and a shot of the victim in the *Globe* today, and it occurred to me maybe I've found our guy. Because it doesn't say "Globe photo by," it just says "Photo by." *Photo by Stan Sloane.*

No answer. I hang up before I get Brendan's voice mail and lose my quarters. I sit in the booth, intending to count to four hundred twenty. Instead I've got this slide show in my head. Stan Sloane in a black anorak under a muted street light on a quiet, potholed road, stands over a body. He inspects it, looking for the age, the gunshot wounds. Speculates about which one was first, which fatal. Careful to avoid stepping in the blood that pools around the torso. His flash angled for stark shadow. The strobe marks the rhythm of the slides changing in my head. This is wigging me out. "Four hundred nineteen," I say out loud. "Four hundred twenty."

This time, Brendan answers.

"Let me ask you something," I say. My ass in its groove on the little booth seat.

"Hello?"

"I thought the point of having a cell phone is that you have it with you. You answer it. I thought that's why people have cell phones."

Brendan has only a cell phone, not a regular phone; he never lives in the same place for long.

"Hello?" Loud this time.

I raise my own voice. "Can you come down here? I'm on to something."

"Oh," he says. "It's you. Where's here?"

"Robert's."

A pause. I hear traffic. "Order me a Murphy's."

I do, then head for the men's room. When I'm out, Brendan has arrived.

I slap the *Globe* in front of him, folded to the page. Stab the photo with my finger. "That's our guy."

Brendan nods. Sips his Murphy's. Foam on his upper lip. "Sure, why not."

I call to Robert, "Got a phone book?"

There are five Stan Sloanes in the Boston white pages. Brendan and I split them. We make a plan to tell him we're the guys he talked to in the bar that afternoon, the Pro Bowlers Tour. How we want to ask him something. It's important. Then we hit the phones. Three Stans we eliminate right away. One has to be a hundred years old, and can't even hear me. A second is a plumber in Revere who thinks I'm playing a practical joke. The third wants to argue about how there's no such thing as a Pro Bowlers Tour. Brendan has left messages on answering machines in Dorchester and Somerville.

Back at the bar. Jazz, a piano player I don't recognize. I make a mental note to ask Robert. Sox muted on the TV, up 5-2 in the seventh.

Brendan spins a coaster on the worn wood. "What next, Marlowe?"

"We wait." It's gotta be close to five. We have an hour at most before the goatee crowd wanders in. We've left the number of the pay phone, and Brendan's cell.

"So the Dog Lady," Brendan says. His mouth doing that little curl it does when he's feeling especially cynical. "I get her on the phone yesterday, she tells me she's decided not to buy the second painting. Needs a different vibe in her office, she says. Embarrassed, but making a joke of it, like we're talking about somebody else. About some force of nature, beyond our control." He sips his Murphy's, like he's done.

"So?"

He shrugs, disgust on his face. "So I remind her, we had a deal - the whole idea of a commission. How I need the money. So get this. *I don't care what we agreed to*, she says. *Things have changed.*"

There you go.

My friend Ramona would be philosophical about this. It was Ramona who once said to me, "Don't go into the desert expecting it to be anything other than the desert." She was talking about the music business, but there's something there for me, too. I'm trying to find some words in that for Brendan, but I can't.

Turns out it's Bud Powell on the bar stereo. "The Roost."

"Good stuff," I say to Robert. "What year?"

Robert has expanded my horizons for jazz. Last year at Christmastime I bought him a Gil Evans box set.

Brendan's reading about the murders. "Yikes. This shit is for real. Seven drug-related murders in the past eight weeks at Cathedral and Bromley-Heath." Brendan is absorbed in the murders, Robert in the game, and I'm stuck on Stan. The money, the intrigue, the risk. *Why does he do it? What does it all mean?*

Three Pru ad guys slide past us (two goatees). Bukowski's is long and narrow, just the bar and some beat-up tables, on a bridge above the Mass Turnpike.

The phone rings out back. Brendan and I look at each other significantly. Even Robert looks over with a kind of grin. I hustle down the hall to the booth, squeak open the door.

"Hello?"

"Thought I might find you there." It's Ramona. There are potentially disturbing implications to her comment, but I let them slide. Because while I'm a little disappointed she's not a Stan, it is good to hear her voice.

"Hey."

"I gotta bail on tonight." We were supposed to go to a movie. "I ran into this guy I used to know. There's possibilities." She's on her cell phone. I can tell because her voice is so clear it starts to break up, like when you speak too closely into a microphone. "Don't hate me."

We make a plan for Saturday night and I go report the no news to Brendan, who's figuring his finances on a bar napkin. He's got nine days to make his rent, and a single-digit bank balance. We hoist our glasses.

"Better days," he says.

Here's why I smashed my cell phone:

I was in talking to Robert one afternoon, having a Newcastle, thinking about how Monk spent all that time holed up in his apartment, and how there was something in that for me, something I was on the verge of getting. I had the phone on the bar, next to my pint.

"What's the thing that makes life vital, Robert?" I said to him. "What gives shape to our existence?"

Robert washed glasses at a little sink under the bar. He raised an eyebrow at me.

"It's having a purpose larger than yourself. A context, where you're part of something. Where you can make a contribution and see it. Think about Monk," I said, trying it out. "It wasn't about music." Robert's eyebrow got higher and his lips got thin. "Or it was, but only because music was the way for him to get to the other thing – the essence." Then my phone rang. I made a little "just a second" gesture with my finger and flipped open the cover.

"Yeah."

"I'm swearing off men, Jack. And this time I mean it." Ramona. My musician. A coincidence not lost on me, but I was on the verge of an epiphany.

"You okay, Ramona?"

"I'm better than okay. I'm resolved."

She didn't sound okay. "I gotta call you back."

I turned to Robert, already losing the thread, where I'd been going with this Monk thing. "This is why we never get to the deep stuff." I held up the phone. "We invite distraction."

Robert dried glasses, a white towel with a green stripe, set them on a rack behind the bar. He nodded. "But can you handle the phone not ringing?"

That night, I took a ball peen hammer and smashed my Nokia.

"Did you know that Dick Weber became an alcoholic late in life?"

Brendan is checking voice mail and only half listening to me. "I did not."

"Think about that," I say.

He puts the phone in his pocket. "Life without bowling too painful to contemplate?"

We're walking down Savin Hill Avenue in Dorchester. Took the Red Line and now we're walking toward the home of the last Stan. I'm getting frustrated. This is a simple concept. "Bowling was incidental. Bowling was not the point."

"So what if this is our Stan? What then?"

A train rumbles past.

"I'm not sure," I say. "Let now be now. And then be then."

"The fuck is that?"

"Wisdom," I say. "Everyday zen."

Brendan was too slow making follow-up calls, so I took over. I was on the verge of pissed, but the Dog Lady/rent situation has been upgraded to crisis, and I've only been doing a rock garden for a marketing consultant out in Wayland. Very yin. Stan number four (Somerville) was amused by our idea, and willing to meet us for a drink, but was not our guy.

We're looking for number nine Doris Street. We turn on Auckland and then left onto Doris and there's a Ryder truck parked and a ramp from the truck to the street and two guys carrying a dresser down the ramp.

We nod solidarity to the dresser guys and check house numbers. Number nine is a triple decker and high off the sidewalk. Major steps. So we make the climb to the small porch and check out the names on the doorbells. Cohen, blank, Gunsallus. No Sloane. We're both sucking wind, and starting to put it together when the dresser guys start doing the first flight of stairs.

"Fuck," I say.

All we can do is wait for them. It's a raw, gray day. The kind we're supposed to be done with by now. Brendan has this red cotton jacket with an International Harvester patch on it and I'm thinking he must be cold. They get to us faster than I'd think. There isn't really room on the porch for four of us plus the dresser, but we make do. The guys are young – twenties – and sweatshirted and dewragged. And one of them has an actual goatee but I'm not going to judge him.

"Moving in?"

The goatee guy nods, catching his breath. He's got a thin face and not much hair. He's wedged between the dresser and the porch railing, but not in a way he's thinking much about.

I gesture at the doorbells. "You know which one's Stan Sloane?"

"Yeah. Mine," he says, and I'm trying to put that together with Cohen-blank-Gunsallus when his friend says, "that's the dead guy."

And I'm either thinking it or I say, "Dead?"

"Yeah. Dead," the first guy says. "That's how I got the apartment."

Brendan's interested. He shoots the Nicholson eye, minus the sneer. "*No.* I mean, you hear about shit like that, but this is the first time..."

"Wait," I say.

"I know," the guy says. "It's like you think it really doesn't happen. Then it does."

"Wait."

"How'd it go down?" Brendan wants to know.

"My friend Scott lives on the first floor. He gave me the landlord's number. I called before he got an ad in the paper."

Brendan nods. Takes out a cigarette. Reaches across the furniture to offer them around.

"Wait," I say. I'm not feeling well. My heart's racing, plus I have this metal taste in my mouth. "Stan Sloane. The dead guy. When? How?"

The goatee guy shrugs. Smokes one of Brendan's Marlboros. "Ten days ago. All I know is it was sudden. Lucky for me, family came and cleared the place out fast. I had a situation."

"Heard that," Brendan says.

We're standing on opposite sides of this dresser, which is long and waist-high, maybe cherry. One corner of it threatens to poke into my thigh. I sneak a look at how it's balanced. One leg touching only air, a second in tenuous contact with the porch. I almost point this out, but I've got slide shows in my head again, Stan Sloane, our Stan Sloane, dead on the sidewalk and some photographer standing over him, taking his picture. I breathe. "You know anything about the guy? Young? Old? Know if he was a photographer?"

A bunch of teens ambushing our Stan as he stands over a body with a camera. They're on him before he knows it, five six of them, knives stab and kicks and a club in the head, and then there's two bodies on the ground.

The guy smokes. "Don't know anything except he lived here, and now he's dead. You knew him?"

"Kind of," I say. "Maybe." I'm trying to deal with the disappointment. The nagging emptiness. Stay jovial and not let on, kicking myself for how I keep believing some epiphany will come, make everything clear. I see Stan leaving a bar, one of the seedy old places in a downtown alley, his face haunted, he's been drinking for courage, undone by his own cynicism. But an exasperated look from Brendan reminds me: how do we know this was our Stan Sloane, or that our guy was *any* Stan Sloane, or that our guy – whoever he was – didn't just make the whole thing up to have a story to tell in a bar on a Tuesday afternoon. I accidentally bump the dresser, and I brace for the bang and scrape, but it doesn't come. I look down. While it appears from my angle that two legs now rest on air and I don't see

124

anyone holding up the far end, no one else is concerned. It's clear to me that there are forces at work in the world I don't understand. I blink away the slide show and Brendan pulls at my sleeve. "Let's go."

But there's a sadness on the goatee guy's face, and it's partly that I'm sad myself and partly that I'm doing whatever it is I do.

"What?" I say, improvising.

And he meets my eyes across the levitating dresser and says, "Death, man. Comes in cycles." He's got those high cheekbones, and an interesting nose. Then his friend's got a hand on his shoulder.

"Dog," the friend says. "Stomach cancer."

And I can see Brendan's eyes roll, like *oh no not dogs*, and the friend says, "George was like fourteen. He was this great, jowly bull-dog."

It's true.

You can't plan these things, or predict them.

Brendan sold the painting that afternoon. Guy loved it. Brendan, under the circumstances and being who he is, wanted to give it to him, but the guy wouldn't hear of it. Wrote a check worth six months rent. He works at the ad agency at the Pru. Go figure.

I don't know what to make of it. Any of it. I try Everyday Zen – "The obstacle *is* the path" – on Robert. But Robert, who's appreciated the irony of the story, isn't impressed with my attempt to affix meaning. He dries glasses on the bar and says, "What about the photographer?"

I shake my head. He doesn't get it. How it's not about the photographer anymore. How it can't be. But that's alright. We've got Monk on the stereo ("Locomotive"), and Brendan's due to call any minute. We're going out to dinner, he and Ramona and I. Brendan's buying. Dog money.

Why I'm Laughing

WATER

Eight years ago, Karen and Lee Holzman had a baby boy named Alex who lived for less than 24 hours, maimed and ultimately defeated by a chromosome disorder. He never left the room he was born in, never breathed the unsanitized air outside the hospital, never saw the nursery whose walls had been carefully stenciled for him with maroon and blue bears. My wife Sarah and I were there, at the hospital. Sarah was Karen's alternate Lamaze coach, and we rushed to Children's Hospital as soon as Lee called to tell us there was trouble. Alex's organs, the doctors said, were incompatible with life.

We watched the digital monitor, all of us, that chronicled the fluctuations of Alex's heartbeat; watched it, I suppose, because it made us feel useful, as if we were helping; watched it because it was easier than watching this child fight for a life we all knew he could not have.

Two things I remember about this. One: Lee, alone with Alex, minutes after Alex had died. I watched him through the glass, and hesitated – I was bringing him something, a cup of water – and I remember looking at my friend, holding his baby in his arms, and feeling so impossibly far away. Two: I remember standing on a hillside in Burbank, under an elm tree, just after the burial, watching people file back to their cars, watching them pass Lee and Karen, offer their tears, their hugs, their support. I remember it was hot, and the sun – so certain, so insistent – seemed incongruous with what had just taken place.

WINDOW SHADE

I've been thinking a lot about family, about the legacies that get passed down, inherited blindly by unsuspecting children whose history explodes inside them as adults, having children of their own, trying to decide what it is they're looking for.

My father was three years old when his father, an interior designer by trade, decided he couldn't handle family life. Went out for ice cream one Saturday night and never came back. Two children at home and a third on the way. A wife six months pregnant who waited until morning to call the police because she suspected what had happened and hoped it would pass – hoped Murray wouldn't get on the train or he would get off at the first stop and hitch a ride back. She could forgive that.

In the morning, when she called the police, Emma found herself hoping he was dead, picturing his bloated body being fished from the Charles River or carried from the scene of an accident, because then she wouldn't have to hate him.

Three months later she died in childbirth, of a hemorrhage which the doctor couldn't stop. When it happened, no one invited Murray back, though everyone – the whole family – knew he was in Nova Scotia, living in a shack at the edge of a farm, painting landscapes on tattered window shades and staying as drunk as he could afford.

What happened instead was this: Murray's brother and sister-in-law took in the kids, all three – my dad, Dorothy and the newborn, Katherine. They had four children of their own and were trying to survive on a railroad man's salary in the days before unions.

Not long after Emma's death, when the time came to claim official custody, Francis, a man whose generosity was matched by a hardness honed through years as an amateur boxer, decided he and

Hannah simply couldn't support seven children, and the only option was to let two of Murray's children go. Dorothy was sixteen, old enough to get a job and contribute. But my dad and the baby were a different story. Hannah objected, but in the end had little choice.

I don't know if my father was told where he was going that day, or why. I only know Francis and Hannah dressed in their Sunday clothes and took my father and his baby sister to the social services office to leave them for adoption. Although I don't know what the room looked like, an impression of it is branded into my genes: wooden chairs, soiled linoleum, and a round clock with a black frame, a white face and stark black numbers. I don't know how long it was before Hannah convinced Francis to come back for them, to reclaim these children, to find a way to make it work. I don't know if it was a matter of minutes or of hours. But after hearing the story, I've never again wondered why my father is so tentative in his expectations of life.

LAUGHTER

My father paints. It's a longtime hobby. Always landscapes, never people. Canvases fill the closets of his large house; they gather dust in the attic. Once in a while he'll give one to a family member who asks, but other than that they remain in storage. I'm a writer, who thinks a lot about the imprint on our lives of incidents we can never know anything about.

My father has never run away. He drinks more than I'm comfortable with, and always has. I remember a few nights when I was a child when he didn't come home and my mom laughed it off, but I wonder what she was really thinking.

REFRIGERATOR

My maternal grandparents' marriage was marked by separate beds, separate rooms, and finally separate sides of the refrigerator.

For many years, they communicated only through the children. He was a conservative German who disapproved of alcohol, of night life, of most things that didn't have to do directly with work and family. My grandmother, it seems, had always felt constrained by him. She liked to go out, visit the clubs, let her hair down. The tension became such that after a few years she dropped all pretense and began to have affairs, frequently, flagrantly. She would disappear for the entire day on Sundays, come home late, and drunk. My grandfather used to sit my mother down and try to cajole her into telling him who my grandmother was with, but my mother didn't know, and didn't realize until years later the intent of the questions or the implications of their answers. My grandfather, who interpreted my mother's lack of information as part of a conspiracy, decided my grandmother had turned the kids against him. Since he believed even less in divorce than he did in drinking, he took his revenge in other ways. He announced one day he would no longer support the family. The left side of the refrigerator was his, and his alone.

My mother was twelve at the time. When she was sixteen, my grandfather was blinded in a chemical accident at a shoe factory in Lowell, and for the remaining three years of his life, had to label his foods on the left side of the refrigerator in braille. As a child, all I knew of this was my grandmother had scrubbed floors on her hands and knees to support the family, and when my parents would go out and she would baby-sit my sister and me, a bottle would come out of the closet and she would begin to tell stories neither of us wanted to hear.

FLOOR TILE

I don't drink. I'm pretty obsessive about my not drinking. I cling to it. And I spend a lot of time thinking about the men in my family and why they've run.

Gene Horton is technically my uncle. He is the father of five of my cousins. I have vague memories of him: a thin, nervous man who played the organ for the local Methodist church. Katherine created a stir when she married him, because she was willing to convert from Catholicism. Mary, her cousin, though they'd grown up as sisters, didn't speak to her for a couple of years. I remember people saying Gene was erratic when he drank, and I remember not knowing what that meant.

When Gene disappeared, it took months before Katherine got a postcard from California. Said I'm sorry. Said I just couldn't handle it. Said I don't expect you to understand.

That was the line – as I sat on the stairs at her house looking at the faces of my cousins, trying to imagine how they must feel – that was the line Katherine laughed at. Good, she said. Then she said, I wouldn't want to disappoint him. The children, for some reason, were all arranged on the stairs. My cousins, my sister, and I. It was a Sunday afternoon. Maureen, the oldest, was eleven. Debbie, the youngest, was three.

Four years later, when she was fifteen, Maureen ran off to Florida with a man who sold floor tile. They got married, but it turned out he was already married to a seventeen-year-old in South Carolina, and he must have smelled trouble because he left half an hour before the police came looking for him. He left Maureen with some bruises and a black leather sample case whose handle had broken.

All five of my cousins became born-again Christians. When I was fourteen, we had Christmas at Mary's house. I wore a Nehru jacket. Gary, who was seventeen, went around asking everyone, "Do you know Jesus as your personal savior?" And if people answered no, he'd say, "Oh," sadness in his voice, then he'd sit quietly for a minute and move on to the next relative.

PERU

Paul lives in a little room at the top of the stairs in a rooming house in western Massachusetts, separated from his wife and son. That's not the way he wants it. She asked him to move out. She wanted more, she said. More excitement. More something. They had moved east from Los Angeles, to this small town outside Worcester, because she wanted to be near her family. He hated to leave L.A. All his friends were there. His career. Not much market for environmental engineers in Massachusetts. But he wanted to keep his family together. A few years ago, on the night Sarah and I nearly separated, Paul showed up for a visit. Brought ice cream. Now he does technical writing, rides the train into Boston every morning, and lives in a small room.

We went for a walk in the woods, in the autumn, in the late afternoon, leaves blanketing the trail, each of us wearing baseball hats.

"She went on a date last night," he told me. "Calls me to see if I'll baby-sit. After telling me I couldn't see Adam the week before." He walked through a shard of sunlight. "So I have to decide. I'm dying to see him, but I feel used. Like she's throwing it in my face."

"What'd you do?"

"Told her no." He shrugged. He scratched the hair under his baseball hat. We bought the hats for a camping trip – Cincinnati Reds and Chicago White Sox. Neither was a team we cared about, but it was all the store had. "Does that seem unreasonable?"

"I stopped trying to be objective a long time ago."

We walked all through Wahconah Falls State Park, following different trails, following the sense of direction we believed would take us back to the car. But when we emerged, it wasn't where we had come in. There was a sign, "Welcome to Peru," and a quiet road that needed repaving. We picked a direction, figuring the road would eventually hook up with the road we were parked on. The sky had clouded over and the wind carried the threat of rain. We covered a few miles before we came across someone we could ask for directions to the park entrance. He was about sixteen, sitting on the front steps of a house, smoking a cigarette. He looked amused. His directions were perfect, and in about two hours, we made it back to the car, just as the sky broke.

All the way home I thought about how many people end up in small rooms. About how, given all that comes between people, it's a miracle anytime things work out.

POTATO SALAD

"You're going to be a father."

Sarah and I, sprawled on the grass at Forest Falls, the San Bernardino Mountains rising behind us, an empty plastic container of German potato salad at our feet, a jug of lemonade nearly empty. She places my hand on her abdomen as she tells me. A dose of physical reality, though it's too early to feel anything. Sarah had insisted on the picnic, had orchestrated the day as she does when she has a surprise in store.

"Well? What do you think?"

We're perched within view of a stream that still carries the runoff from the snow and ice melting in the mountains beyond us. She has just finished telling me about a time, she was in junior high, walking home from school in the rain, her yellow rain slicker keeping her dry. The rain got so heavy she lost her bearings. Couldn't find her way home on a route she walked every day. Now my hand is on her belly.

We both love to be near water. I listen to the sound of the stream flowing, feel the nothing that is a something growing inside of her, and I laugh.

She slaps my arm. "What?" she says.

Maybe it's the potato salad. Maybe it's the lemonade. Maybe it's the sheer impossibility that we, who get lost walking through the woods, who cannot find our way home in the rain, could ever take care of anyone. I can't stop myself.

BROTHER

Two years after Alex's death, Karen and Lee had another baby. A healthy girl named Rachel, who likes plastic frogs, cloth books and stuffed zebras. Karen and Lee planned to tell Rachel about Alex. They just wanted to wait for the right time, find the right way to explain to her how she both was and wasn't an only child. The summer Rachel turned four, we were sitting around their living room one night, drinking iced tea and listening to Rachel tell us about her day. She told us about finding her brother, about going for a walk along the dirt road that ran through the apple orchard, how he joined her, how he taught her things as she played. There was an awkward moment. We all looked at one another, each waiting for someone else to react. Rachel looked up at her parents, fresh from spinning her story. Karen broke the silence.

"Does he live near here?"

Rachel tapped her head. "Here."

The tips of Lee's ears turned red against his black hair. "Rachel, you had a brother once. His name was Alex."

Rachel looked around the room as if trying to find him. She smiled at her mother, suspecting a trick was being played. "Where is he?"

Karen picked her daughter up and held her in her lap. "He had a disease. He didn't live long. Less than a day."

Rachel's lips puckered. She squinted her eyes. "What was he like?"

I watched the faces of my friends as they searched for a way to answer their daughter's question. Karen looked at Lee, studying his face, his head. It was a full minute or more before she managed to say, "He had dark hair. Like his father."

The Encyclopedia of (Almost) all the Knowledge in the World

HE CAME TO US FROM GERMANY, after a long and unre-warded life serving the courts of various kings, rulers whose names many of us knew from history books, names we associated with the great tide of human existence, names we never dreamed would be in any way connected to our lives. He came by accident, this man whose work we had studied at the wooden desks of our childhood. Leibniz, the near-great mathematician, denied the recognition he believed he deserved because, at the same time he was developing the differential calculus, a man named Isaac Newton was one step ahead of him. He came to us in his later years and, some may have thought, with his best work behind him. He came as a man who believed he had learned to put the accolades of others in perspective. And he came as an outcast, unwanted by his own people.

Leibniz, by the time he came to us, was not the imposing figure many of us might have imagined. A stoop-shouldered man with ill-fitting false teeth and a penchant for clashing plaids, he moved among us quietly and unobtrusively at first, hoping merely to be a good citizen. But some people, it seems, cannot content themselves with the common round, and no matter how much they profess, and even believe in, their desire for the simple life, the urge to do something great eats at them, and it becomes only a question of time and the particular idea that will seize their imagination.

So it was with Leibniz. He had fallen out of favor in Germany under the reign of George Louis, a humorless man who suffered from the gout and who would not tolerate anyone in his employ who had hair. Leibniz' flowing mane of red hair thus became his Achilles' heel, as the despot demoted the celebrated mathematician, thinker and statesman to court historian. Leibniz, who had spent years ruminating on his fate of playing second fiddle to Isaac Newton, began to speculate: if two men could be at work on the same task for years, never knowing the other existed, couldn't the same be true of civilizations? He began to wonder about parallel universes, societies where discoveries were potentially being made equal to or beyond the ken of a statesman in the closed society of a European monarchy in the height of the Victorian era. So he commissioned a ship to be built at the cost of the kingdom, and set sail for the unknown, for whatever he might find in the way of vindication.

Leibniz later confessed to us his original intent, upon finding some lost civilization, was to appropriate a discovery and return to Germany to garner the acclaim he had earlier been denied. However, in his twelve years at sea, he found no lost races, no hidden peoples, no reputation-making artifacts, though he did find many friends and several good local brews. He also told us that along the way he found humility, a desire to settle down among a people who would accept him as he was. So it was that twelve years after he left his native land, a changed Leibniz set sail for Constantinople, with two guides in tow, as well as an apprentice navigator not fully devoted to his craft. At crucial points of the journey, the neophyte steersman read the charts upside down, so that the ship eventually ended up being sighted off our shores, and Leibniz was welcomed immediately as a citizen, for we have always been supporters of higher mathematics.

In his first days here he talked of learning a trade, possibly fishing, for he found the sea air refreshing. But it wasn't long before his mind turned to greater things. Perhaps the first indication that the confines of rural life were weighing him down was an increasingly relentless questioning of everyone he met about the source of the differential. "Who do you know as the discoverer of the calculus?" he would ask in his curious voice, half whine, half lisp, his head tilted to one side like a top-heavy egg, his false teeth rattling in his mouth as he spoke. And when the unsuspecting citizen whom Leibniz had corralled would answer Newton, the embittered sage would spit, "Fiend. Usurper. Half-wit. Pedestrian."

The second indication that something big was brewing in the distended caverns of Leibniz's brain was his creation of a calculator able to extract roots, multiply and divide as well as add and subtract. It wasn't long after he sold the patent for the calculator to an enterprising young businessman named Casio, that Leibniz appeared before us rejuvenated, scrubbed and shaved, drained once again of his anger, and began talking to everyone he met about something he called the Universal Characteristic, a language in which all truths could be expressed and in which the names were to reveal the character of the objects. He planned to compile this into a book that contained all knowledge, so disputes would be impossible.

We certainly share the responsibility for what happened. We encouraged him. We were accustomed to strange notions and grandiose visions; they seem to be our legacy and heritage, and we have always supported them as much from a desire to see people happy as from a belief in the limitless possibilities of human achievement. So when Leibniz began talking, we listened, and told him his idea sounded wonderful, partly because it did, for who wouldn't marvel at such a notion, and partly because it made him happy to consider it, and we much preferred a happy Leibniz to the one that had been moping and raging around for months.

Watching him undertake the work was a spectacle. He dipped into a treasury none of us knew he had, pilfered from the coffers of Germany's tyrant king, and purchased a row of byzantine warehouses built during the time of the twentieth Edwin B.'s architectural smorgasbord. He began interviewing prospective knowledge gatherers, and spent months checking references and probing the historical understanding of some of our more ambitious young minds in the vast, unfinished corridors of his newly renovated home. He commissioned three ships, built of the finest wood, and christened them Learning, Virtue and Piety for reasons none of us quite understood. He purchased pallet upon pallet of paper and had it stored out of the way, waiting. He purchased enormous drums of ink in every color of the rainbow.

Finally, when all else was ready, when all the preparations were made and all his helpers hired, he built the calculator that would tabulate it all. The size and shape of an enormous pipe organ, it had a separate key for every possible sound, another for every conceivable shape, and a set of foot pedals that covered all nuance. He built it of petrified wood so he would never have to concern himself with it breaking down in mid-stride, and the keys he connected with an elaborate gear and pulley system through which three sheets of paper always moved. These then hooked onto a conveyor which would channel them into three separate, identical warehouses where the great man's tireless legions would begin the arduous process of cataloguing each new piece of information as it came off the printer. The calculator, when completed, stretched near the top of the highest dome in the largest warehouse, and its machinations could be heard for blocks around.

And so the work began. Knowledge gatherers of the top rank launched the ships Learning, Virtue and Piety in search of obscure intelligence from remote quadrants of the earth. Others combed the libraries for every iota of wisdom about their assigned subject. Volunteers from the village assisted the headquarters to tell what they knew to other gatherers who served primarily as reporters. And Leibniz himself set to work tabulating what he knew off the top of his head, which kept him busy for the first couple of weeks until other research started coming in.

There were those in the village who were skeptical from the start. Some felt such an undertaking was blasphemy, and for the first few days a small group of protesters paced in front of the main warehouse with signs saying, "Only God Can Know Everything," and "Leibniz's Tower of Babble," but the whirring and whining of the machinery assaulted their eardrums and in the course of a few days, overcame their zeal, so they took to merely badmouthing the project from afar. Others simply thought it foolish, fruitless, the equivalent of trying to determine the volume of water in the sea. They feared the project would damage our credibility with the provisional government and endanger our school funding, though it never came to that.

For the most part, there was either enthusiastic support or quiet tolerance. Our downtown area had been deserted for generations, since the ghost of the twentieth Edward B. had driven all business and residence away with his persistent demands for renovation, so most of us were happy to see the buildings in use again, and willing to make minor adjustments in our habits to accommodate the project. Generally we could avoid the area without any trouble, and those who had to go in took to wearing ear muffs as protection against the noise.

Leibniz and his staff grew accustomed to it. It seemed neither to bother them nor disturb their hearing. The project's employees quickly evolved into two camps: those who quit and those who became devoted followers of Leibniz, firm adherents of his idea, as though there were something in the air of the warehouse, in the persistent hum of the machinery, that got under the skin and into the brain and created zealots. This all happened in the span of a few weeks, so the bespectacled German was quickly down to a core crew of devoted workers whose efforts he could trust completely. They became identifiable among us for their pallid complexions, their polite manners, and the slightly demented glow of the believer in their eyes.

138

By the end of that first month, Leibniz had perfected a system and holed up in his laboratory, the giant vaulted cathedral which contained his beautiful calculating machine. From time to time, Learning, Virtue or Piety would return, its small crew haggard from a voyage among the Watachichi Indians of Maori, or a sojourn among a tribe of pig farmers on a small island south of Zanzibar, and sit in a cluster around Leibniz, telling their stories and eating together like an ancient war council, Leibniz working the keys and pedals of his great machine ceaselessly, occasionally smiling at some nugget of wisdom he heard.

Once all the lore from all the villagers and all the data from the libraries had been gleaned, the teams of knowledge gatherers, this staff of disciples, would bring in every new piece of information as soon as it was realized, and another group would sort through these bits to determine which were true, which were false, and which were merely different ways of saying the same thing. Leibniz would take these bits of knowledge and dutifully tabulate them until every one was determined both in its essence and in its relationship to every-thing else, so every object, every notion, every concept would be able to be clearly articulated and understood, with the disadvantage that, because the name of each piece of knowledge also contained its rela-tion to all others, even the most simple names took years to say or to read, and the most complex notions, such as the knowledge of God, would take all of human history, past, present and future, to say, and all the paper and ink that ever was or ever will be to write down, so that while it was theoretically possible not only to prove God's exis-tence but to know him, no one person could live long enough to even speak his own name.

But Leibniz continued his work, undaunted, striving always to find short cuts that would enable people to greet each other in less than a lifetime or to know they were alive before they died, and his disciples continued to diligently tear from the calculator the endless reams of paper containing the endless names of endless pieces of data, and to pass them to other followers who would catalogue the entries in strict numerical order, and pass them in turn to other followers who would place the revised entries into the revised volume of the encyclopedia of (almost) all the knowledge in the world, who would in turn pass this volume to other followers who would distribute each revised edition to the libraries and bookstores where people would come out of curiosity, though of course no one ever read the entire work, and few even understood any part of it.

As it became increasingly clear the task Leibniz had set for himself was impossible, the naysayers among us began to snicker with the self-righteousness of the safe, of people who never take risks and scoff at those who do. Most, however, were impressed by the effort itself, by the ingeniousness of the idea, the faithfulness with which Leibniz and his staff carried it through, and the sheer spectacle of the work in progress. For Leibniz had created an impressive, if incomplete, volume that represented the panorama of human thought perhaps more fully than anything before or since. An abridged version of the book, which catalogued all knowledge but ignored the interrelationships, sold well for a time, but Leibniz had it pulled from the shelves when he heard of people using it to jump to conclusions and commit other irrational acts.

Despite his frustrations and the overwhelming tide of evidence that completion of the task was impossible, Leibniz worked on, obsessive, and throughout the years of his labor refused to accept the fact there would come for him no moment, no nanosecond of history where the flow of paper would cease, the frantic activity of his followers pause, the wild gyrations of his gears and pulleys and the ululating shrieks of the machinery that always, inevitably, needed oil, momentarily be silenced, no infinitesimal fragment of time evolve where the flow of information would stop and he could believe, for one glorified moment, a parenthesis in the sentence of the years, that he knew all there was to be known. Even though he could never have proved it, he would have been satisfied, and it was this hope that fueled him, enabled him to work nineteen hours a day, seven days a week for thirty-four years without so much as a coffee break.

In the end, it was logistics that did him in, the most mundane of concerns, the most prosaic of problems. Money. The well ran dry. His followers, who were willing to continue the project despite its hopelessness, simply because they enjoyed the work and could no longer envision a life for themselves apart from it, nonetheless had to eat, and Leibniz could no longer feed them. He could no longer afford the paper or ink to feed through his machine, nor the provisions to send his ships in search of increasingly exotic cultures. True to his vision, Leibniz did not allow the operation to peter out, selling first one piece, then another, laying off one group at a time, slowly dwindling the flow of information to a trickle. When he could no longer finance the entire project, he rested his fingers on the keyboard and called the whole thing to a halt.

The silence startled the workers, upon whom realization started slowly, and spread like a virus, which is what they thought they had contracted, so radical was this sudden cessation of sound. Even those walking downtown when it happened were disoriented by the absence of the noise that had been part of our world for over three decades. Leibniz, who had calculated the financial statement in a moment of down time on his enormous machine, simply turned in his seat, adjusted his wire-frame glasses on his bird-like nose, looked out at the frozen faces of his shocked workers and said, "We can no longer continue. Thank you all very much," and walked to his long neglected bedroom to sleep.

When he emerged a week later, it was with two suitcases packed, his hair neatly combed and tied in a small ponytail at the back of his head, his trousers and tunic a horrendous clashing of green and brown plaids. He also had an announcement. "I'll be leaving at sunset," he told the small crowd that had gathered, surprised and a little curious at his emergence, since the news of his bankruptcy had traveled fast and we spent a great deal of time speculating about what he might do next. "I've very much enjoyed my stay here, and appreciate your hospitality and kindness at taking me in as one of your own. But I must go, because it is in my nature to find adventure." And with that, he picked up his bags, walked toward Virtue, which had remained the most seaworthy of his three ships, climbed aboard and disappeared into the hold. True to his word, as the sky began to darken and the sun to be swallowed by the sea, he set sail to the south, taking three of his most devoted cohorts with him, along with several barrels of provisions we had collected for him that afternoon.

Only his own lofty expectations kept the work a secret and keep Leibniz a relative unknown to this day, deprived of the recognition he so desperately sought. In a simple ceremony before leaving the city, this great thinker, this worshipper of wisdom, burned his notes along with all copies of all editions of the text, believing if it couldn't exist with the hope of perfection, then it was a failure and must be destroyed. Thus was the world deprived of its first and greatest encyclopedia, the most comprehensive volume of human knowledge ever compiled. Despite that, Leibniz remains among us a noble reputation. His calculator, the colossal machine built of petrified wood, is our most popular tourist attraction, and remains a testament to Leibniz and the grandiosity of his vision.

Over the Falls

1.

MICHELLE IS GETTING A DIVORCE. David has finally moved out. Got an apartment north of Toronto. This choice a dozen years in the making. Realizing the marriage would not could not work. Realizing David's troubles were in fact clinical, though he would not acknowledge them as such. Feeling she should stay and help him through - that to leave a sick man was cruel.

Here's what finally happened. David wanted to go for a drive, and wanted to take the kids with him. He believed Jesus was going to meet him in the Foodarama parking lot, that he would climb aboard an airplane bound for heaven. He wanted the kids – Dan and Lucy – to come.

"We are adjusting," Michelle says. "Pretty peaceful," she says. A pause. "And not at all. Who am I kidding."

This is not the first time something like this has happened. It's just the first time in a long time David has failed to acknowledge it as illness. Michelle had made David promise he wouldn't take the kids out when he was feeling sick. Had made him promise he would tell her when he was experiencing symptoms. Had vowed to leave with the kids if he ever broke that pledge.

"Mental fucking illness," Michelle says. "I'm sorry, did I say that?"

2.

Michelle and David went to college together. From the day they met, David believed God wanted them to be married. Michelle was dating someone else, who wasn't ready to get serious. Michelle was. She was flattered by David's intensity, drawn to his certainty. We were all part of the same church group, a college fellowship in a big, established church. David tended to hear from God in the way a lot of us did. A leading of the spirit. An inclination.

Now it's almost twenty years later. Michelle has two teenage children and lots of lingering questions about faith. About David. Michelle and I talk a lot on the phone. She and my wife Anna as well. She needs to talk to people who support her decision. Her home church does not believe in divorce. Plus, people there are not fully convinced David is sick. For one thing, Michelle does not tell them of the incidents. She knows how they sound. She doesn't want people thinking badly of David.

Two years ago, David had been driving along the interstate, taking Lucy to camp. By Lucy's account, they were having a good time. Everything was fine. They'd stopped for cheeseburgers and milk shakes. Talked about the marvel of the human circulatory system, which she was studying in school. A quiet stretch of road, when the conviction came over David that Jesus was coming for him. He saw distant lights, across a field at the side of the road, and steered the car toward them.

3.

The Bible, of course, is filled with stories of people who heard from God. People who were not mentally ill. Consider Abraham, who left behind everything, taking his wife in search of a land God promised him.

There's lots more. But the one who intrigues me is Zechariah. Supporting role in the Christmas story. Husband to Mary's cousin Elizabeth. Priest in God's temple. Father (eventually) of John the Baptist. But there's the sticking point.

Because at the time the story finds them, Zechariah and Elizabeth are old. They've never been able to have a child. Then one day Zechariah's in the temple, preparing incense. And an angel who calls himself Gabriel comes to him, tells him he's going to have a son. After an understandable moment of hesitation, Zechariah asks a question: *how shall I know this for certain?*

And is rendered mute. *Because,* the angel says, *you did not believe my words.*

4.

"I had a dream we visited you," Michelle tells me. "You and Dan went out somewhere and the two of you came back with a puppy. I got lost in your kitchen closet, and met a man inside the walls of your house. We sat and talked for a long time."

Anna and I are both on the line. Conferenced in. I'm at my office downtown, looking out my tenth-story window at the construction site across Summer Street. Steel girders and concrete. Where twice in the last hour a port-a-potty has sailed by, hoisted toward the upper floors. Anna's in her car. It's good to hear her breathing.

Michelle lives in Woodbridge, near Toronto. We don't see each other nearly as often as we'd like. Our daughters are pals, despite an age gap. Michelle and her kids have been spending a lot of time at Niagara Falls, she tells us. She has become fascinated by the stories of the people who've gone over the falls in barrels. Those who made elaborate preparations. Those who just hurled themselves into the void.

"Annie Taylor," she tells us. "She was the first. A school teacher. Airtight wooden barrel. Compressed the pressure with a bicycle pump after she got in. She lived. Barely. And when she emerged, bruised and battered, she said *nobody ought ever to do that again.*"

Anna and I are quiet. We're neither of us sure how to respond to this; each, I suspect, hoping the other will find something to say.

But it's Michelle who speaks next. "We've all got to choose what truth we hold onto," she says. "We're all hurling ourselves over some falls in a barrel. So it can't be about being right. We've got to hope grace finds us."

5.

Okay, here it is: Zechariah's reaction to the angel strikes me as reasonable. Think about it. A man spends a good chunk of his life praying for his heart's desire: a son. He believes God is bigger than his wife's infertility, his own impotence, the chemical reaction between him and her that results in no spark of life. He prays, every day. Five years. Ten. Twenty. There comes a point he has to make a decision. To surrender. To accept the evidence of his faithful experience and come to a different understanding of God. That God does not grant to everyone their deepest yearning. Maybe he scales back his expectations. Maybe, over time, he comes to think of it as arrogance that any of us would ever expect God to grant our wishes. Maybe, through years of soul searching, he comes to define faith as a loving, steadfast response to what God brings your way. Maybe, in the way he works through this disappointment, nourishing his spirit so the sadness becomes fertile soil for maturity rather than bitterness, maybe in doing this the priest Zechariah is an inspiration to his congregation. Maybe this journey itself is the very evidence and substance of his faith, and while there is a part of him that still yearns for a miracle, he is fulfilled in his life. His service to God. Then, one day, as he's preparing incense in the temple, an angel appears.

6.

"This is still a city where an artist can afford to live. I'd love to buy one of these buildings, vast studio space. You guys could come do it with me."

We're in a coffee shop on Elmwood Avenue in Buffalo. Michelle and Anna and I at a table drinking hot chocolate on a February afternoon. Lucy and our daughter Megan are next door looking at used CDs.

The place is jammed on a Saturday. Michelle looks older than the last time I saw her. Crow's feet. Streaks of gray. "Of course I'd prefer he had stayed at his parents. But that wasn't going to last." Michelle and the kids are staying at the house. They were more comfortable when David was three hours east, at his parents house. It's not that they believe he'll be violent. It's that they don't know what to believe. We've been to the Albright-Knox Museum. Played "hat or hairdo."

"We're going to have to do this in the courts. I'm going to be up there trying to convince them he's a danger to us. To the kids. His doctors won't support that. And I don't know if I've got the stomach."

"You can do it. People will help you." Anna has an important role in this. She's the only one grounded enough to stay practical. Focus on what needs to be done. Believe the system can work for you. It had been her idea that we come to Buffalo for a visit.

Megan and Lucy come through the door. I've never adjusted to seeing my daughter from a distance. Unexpectedly. Sometimes I think it's only in those moments that I really see her. As a person, apart from me. So here they are. Bursting breath. Dueling blondes.

"Look what we found," Lucy says. "Wild Colonials." Lucy is applying to colleges. She's an avid - and outstanding - fencer. Michelle says Lucy is the most focused person she knows. "I'm going to burn a copy for Megan before they go." They're laughing at something, and then they're off. They see each other once a year, they're five years apart in age, and they're friends. I marvel.

Elmwood Avenue is Buffalo's funky street. It feels like somewhere we could live. Anna and I have been thinking about moving somewhere less expensive. So we could spend less energy running just to make ends meet. We need to adjust our course, but we don't know how. We're confronted every day by our limitations, our narrow band of capabilities.

Lucy and Megan are back. They've plunked themselves into chairs before I realize they've returned. Michelle is looking at Lucy and you can tell she's thinking her girl will be leaving before long.

"What'cha talking about?" Lucy asks.

"Oh, you know."

Lucy rolls her eyes. "Come on, Mom." She clutches the Wild Colonials CD. "Repeat after me. A complex system can give rise to turbulence and coherence at the same time."

Michelle says it. Then she says, "Chaos theory. They're studying it in school."

7.

"Now the Lord said to Abraham, 'go forth from your country, and from your relatives and from your father's house, to the land which I will show you…' So Abraham went forth as the Lord had spoken to him."

— Genesis 12:1-4

There are all kinds of faith, I know. Believing you hear God. Acting in obedience to certain principles, like the ten commandments. Confidence in some system of natural rules or laws. At one end of the spectrum, you've got Abraham, a story that's bedrock for me. At the other, you've got someone like Red Hill Jr.

In the summer of 1951, Red Hill Jr. planned to go over the falls in a contraption made from 13 inner tubes held together with fish net and canvas straps. On August 5, Hill climbed into the thing and plunged into the rapids. Even before his contrivance reached the falls, it began to come apart. Tossed in the air, thrown from side to side, caromed off rocks. Hill and his device disappeared into the mist and roiling water. The next day, his body was pulled from the river.

8.

Before she took action, Michelle had asked us to ask our pastor for counsel.

Mari, before she was a pastor, worked in a crisis counseling center. We sat, Mari and Anna and I, in Mari's office.

"Tell her she needs to leave," Mari said, without hesitation, when she'd heard the story.

"Okay," I said. "Yes. But where's the line between faith and madness. What about the whole idea of people legitimately hearing from God?"

"If the women had been in charge back in the Old Testament, things would have been very different," Mari said.

Anna nodded.

"Wait," I said. "Abraham. Great act of faith. Heading into the desert because God told him to."

Mari's face wore an inscrutable smile. She looked at Anna, as if the two of them shared some understanding that was utterly lost on me. "All I'm saying, if he'd listened to Sarah, things would have been different."

9.

We are people who value the ineffable, Anna and I. Who believe the truly essential in life is not adequately accounted for by reason alone.

We have a good marriage, by all accounts. We're a team. We love each other, we've got a terrific kid, and what appears to be a 10-year itch cycle. We had a major blow-up at the ten-year mark, and another last year. These storms come out of nowhere, and they're bad. The first time we split for nearly a year. Last time I slept on a friend's floor for a week and looked into getting my own place. A week later, we were okay.

We've had to figure out our own take on faith over the years, as anyone does. To watch some of our own deepest desires – a second child, a political career – not come to pass. We live in a world where port-a-potties fly through the air, suspended on cables from giant cranes. Who are we to say anything is impossible. And yet, we have grown skeptical about people who hear from God. We have our reasons. But we've lost something in that evolution. A part of the faith experience that's beyond our borders. We're attuned to God's voice – if at all – only in quiet ways. Sometimes I get sad about that, and I remind myself: we're broken, all of us somehow, and maybe the human condition is such that when grace finds us, if it does, we can only receive it in shards. Our *thank you* inevitably muted by the scars of our experience.

Mile Marker 283

THIS IS HOW IT BEGINS: IT'S COLD. There's a dusting of snow on the sides of the road and a thick, erratic white line, a ghosted imprint that maps where salt has melted ice. A fine powder hovers an inch or two above the asphalt, blown back and forth by a constant wind. A wind that swirls around the cab of the truck. A truck that carries a trailer whose battered gray metal contains, whose corrugated sides protect, a load of pecans (twenty-two tons of pecans, harvested in Duncan, North Carolina and loaded in Raleigh, the pecans released down an aluminum chute, the sound like a stampede, the whole thing, the actual loading, taking no more than a minute). In the cab of the truck, behind the wheel, is where Ellen sleeps. Soon she will wake, and wonder where she is.

"Tuesday, December 10. Pulled over at 4:45 am on I-87 in Hudson, NY on the way to Montreal with a load of pecans."

Ellen's eyes blink open and immediately focus on the note attached to the tiny clip on the steering wheel. She stares at the words, concentrating on breathing slowly, until the information registers. She takes a deep breath. The paper is yellow, a three-inch by five-inch Post-It note written on in blue ink. It is a habit. A precaution against forgetting, which has happened to her before. Which she has structured her life to prevent from happening again. The clip is metal, and

151

screwed into the hub of the steering wheel, which is black and hard plastic, smooth and familiar, because every inch of its circumference has been shaped to the contours of Ellen's fingers, worn to her touch.

It is home.

It is the first thing she touches when she wakes in the cab of her truck. Always.

She looks through the windshield at pre-dawn light bleeding over the frozen highway. At the traces of snow that grace the sides of the road like dust, the moisture seemingly frozen out of them. It's hard to imagine anything melting, anything becoming liquid again in this cold. It's the kind of cold that comes close to registering as memory for Ellen. But a different cold grows inside her now. Her head. Her chest. Her legs. Her fingers. This cold scares her. Makes her lose hold.

She looks at her watch, a Swatch that Bernie gave her, with black numbers and luminous hands on a white face. 6:15. It will be light soon. There are spots of water on the windshield, apparently from melted snow. There are words on the note, words she needs, words she has not needed before but now needs. To tell her where she is. To bring her back from wherever she has been.

The truck's cab is warm. The fan is on "2," the temperature set all the way over to red. There is an AM radio and CB mounted in the dash, its microphone tucked neatly away. Usually it is on the seat, at Ellen's side, but it has a short and has worked only sporadically since Virginia. Ellen will need to get it fixed. The brown leather bench seat is warm to her touch. She never wears gloves to drive. She likes the feel of the wheel on her hands, the stick shift knob, same smooth black plastic molded to her touch. It is part of the iconography that lets her know she is she. The simplicity of this world. Her world.

Here's how Ellen and Bernie got to be friends: they met in the elevator of their Inman Square apartment building, each coming home from work, and introduced themselves. Then Ellen said, "I have a cat named Bernie."

Ellen's eyes return to the note on her steering wheel. Register the information. She can feel her blood circulating. Feel it feeding her brain. She takes a deep breath.

There is a feeling that something has happened which she should remember. There is a certainty that she should have remembered where she is. What's in her truck. There is a foreboding that makes her hands cold. There is a sound, like crying.

Her eyes are drawn to a single headlight approaching in the opposite direction, across the Thruway. The headlight illuminates a spot at the edge of Ellen's consciousness, where something small hovers. But Ellen doesn't get enough of a glimpse to see what it is, or even to be sure she saw something. The car passes, and the Thruway is again dark.

Inside her head, Ellen hears the sound that sounds like crying, that may be crying, and thinks about the something she thinks might have happened. The something she can't remember. A report on the radio? She tells herself her need for the words on the note to locate her is simply an indication of interrupted sleep. But Ellen is accustomed to interrupted sleep.

"It's not so strange," Ellen told Bernie. "Sleep for me is not one unbroken line. It is line segments, stacked on top of one another. The sum turns out the same as most people's, it's just the form that's different." Ellen likes invoking elementary school math. Before she drove truck, she taught fourth grade. Bernie is the only friend of Ellen who understands the sleep thing. Who supports her career change.

Imagine a baby in a basket, in blankets. Left by the side of a road, say a rest stop on a highway, say in early summer. The baby, no more than a few weeks old, has been abandoned. There is no note, no way to know the child has been abandoned except for the realization that no parent would have forgotten a child by the side of the road. It is

153

impossible to imagine any parent forgetting to put the child back in the car and driving off.

Here's why Ellen likes Bernie: Bernie used to be terrified of heights. So on his 30th birthday he jumped out of an airplane. Figured the sky diving would kill him or cure him. Ellen can understand this sort of behavior. It's why she now drives truck. It has to do with the sleeping thing. With her need to control it, so she can function. The inability to remember details, important details, when she wakes up, is a sign she is losing control. It has happened before. She lost her teaching job because of it, and she has taken to driving truck as a way to force herself to beat it. As a challenge of discipline. And it has worked. Until now.

Dawn has begun to creep across the landscape. She has a vague sense of having come from North Carolina, though she can't remember if it was this trip or last. She has a paycheck in her pocket. She has a feeling that she's forgetting something. That there is a picture she can't get into the front part of her brain. In the back part of her trailer, she's fairly certain she's carrying a brokered load.

There are days when Ellen simply can't stay awake for more than a few hours at a time. "It's been like this since I was a kid," she said to Bernie the night she told him about it. "As far back as I can remember."

They were in the Border Cafe in Harvard Square, eating nachos and drinking margaritas, and Ellen was telling Bernie, who has a cat named Elmo, about her plans for a career change, and the reasons. Ellen has green eyes and tremendous peripheral vision. Ellen held a tortilla chip in her left hand and poked it into and out of the guacamole. She loved teaching, but she had come unmoored. Lost the ability to push her body to the end of class, to the secret nap breaks that had sustained her.

"The other day," she said, "I woke up, on my feet, in front of the class, a Venn diagram on the board." She drew on a napkin with a felt tip pen two overlapping circles and shaded the common area with diagonal lines. "Like this. At first I had no idea where I was or why these children were staring at me. I didn't know if I'd been out for a few seconds or a few minutes. They had their chins in their hands, that late morning funk. Some of them wouldn't notice if I left and the others are too polite to say anything."

Bernie smiled. Bernie was making a significant dent in the beans and cheese side of the plate of nachos.

Bernie works designing computer chips in an office with one-way glass so competitors can't see in. A building on Route 128 in Waltham. Bernie will go on work jags, seven eight nine days at a stretch, non-stop, when he gets into a project. Then he'll take a few days off to sleep.

Sleep is what scares Ellen right now. The possibility that she has come unmoored. That she will blink and find herself somewhere else. Twenty-two tons of momentum behind her. She wraps her fingers around the steering wheel.

"I've been thinking about black holes," Ellen says into her micro-cassette recorder, which is a Sony, which, like Bernie, is a name she trusts. She bought the tape recorder because she likes communicating with Bernie and he likes hearing what she has to say. It is a way for her to anchor herself. To make the circles of her life overlap. Bernie plays the tapes while he's on his work jags. Ellen likes to think of Bernie designing microchips while she speaks into her microcassette recorder, often about physics, which is something she has begun to regret not studying. Bernie likes to think of Ellen driving on high-ways throughout the northeast while he listens to the tapes, sealed in his office with one-way glass. Ellen says into the tape recorder, "How amazing it is something can exist that is made up of a whole bunch of not existing. How so much nothing becomes a something."

155

Ellen also likes carrying the microcassette recorder because she can't say things like this into her CB.

Into her CB she has to say things like, "Recycler, this is Baby Driver. You copy?"

And Recycler, who is a base, a retired man who sits in his home and stays at his radio late into the night to act as an information source and a communication companion to travelers, Recycler will say things like, "Welcome back, Baby Driver," which is Ellen's handle, and "What's your twenty?" which means where are you, what's your location.

And although sometimes, when Ellen has just awakened, she would like to answer, "the event horizon," and talk about black holes, instead she will say, "Coming up on Exit 12," which will mean she is just outside Malta, New York. And Recycler, who lives in Ballston Spa, will chat with her for a few minutes while she's in range – newsy stuff, anything – and it will help keep her awake, help keep her connected. Now all her strategies are in question, because she needed the words on the note to tell her where she was.

Imagine a baby in a basket. In blankets. Imagine the baby near a stream. At its edge. Put a cow in the picture, grazing in the distance. This is, of course, a ridiculous picture. And Ellen knows this, but this is the picture she has in her mind, the picture that keeps returning to her mind now she has awakened. The picture that formed in her mind from words she believes she heard on the radio, about a baby found on a farm nearby. She thinks in Hudson Falls. She thinks she heard this, but she can't be sure. To be sure something happened she has to be able to reconstruct in her head the moment of the experience, to rebuild it and watch it unfold again. But when she reconstructs a moment of turning on the radio in her cab and hearing about a baby abandoned on a farm, it doesn't feel familiar. The information feels right. A baby, in a basket, on a farm. She feels something pulling at her, drawing her toward it. She fears that it is sleep. That it will take her over.

Ellen turns on the radio and scans the AM dial for news among the sounds of country music, radio preachers and insistent static that attacks her speakers. "Pataki said today –*SQUAAAAWK* – expects the bill to get through the House and – *DZZZIPZIPP* – desk within a week. Anything else, he said, would suggest – *HSSSSSSSS* – *FFUL-LZZZOP*." Like hands rubbing hard against a balloon. Ellen tries to concentrate on the words. Listens for sounds about a farm. A baby. But the words that do come arrive as if from far away, like messages intercepted from space. And the next story, as far as she can tell, is about a welfare reform bill, and after that news of a pending storm interrupted by a squawk so loud and so long it makes Ellen's head hurt and she turns the radio off.

Ellen has thought about falling in love with Bernie. She would like to fall in love. She would like to have someone in addition to her cat to come home to on those two or three nights every few weeks when she comes home. Bernie seems well-suited in temperament and schedule, so she has considered falling in love with Bernie. She is fond of Bernie. She likes being with him. She has said to Bernie, "Maybe these emotions are as near to love as love will ever be," and Bernie has said, "Isn't that a Paul Simon lyric?" and they have both laughed and that is as far as it has gone.

Or this: There is a report on the radio. A baby found in a basket, by a river, on a farm, in Hudson Falls. There is a baby in a basket. There is a paycheck in Ellen's pocket. The two facts seem unrelated. The two circles do not overlap.

She re-checks her watch, making sure the date says 10, not 11. It's one of the things that happens when she comes unmoored. Sleeping right through. Not knowing. She hates the not knowing.

Know this about Ellen. Ellen dreams in pictures. Locations. Many of them recurring locations, like these:

A stream, nearly frozen over, just small circular clear spots where water can be seen flowing, eddying, living beneath the ice; a wooden bridge, a walking bridge, over the stream, an inch or so of snow packed on its surface; the sound of the water and the sound of the wind.

A field, also covered with snow, and a road running through it, the snow on it packed, tire tracks, footprints, but still covered, the white unbroken except for the brown-gray of an old barn in the distance and the wisps of sticks and branches tall enough to reach above the snow here and there. She imagines it as Vermont, but she has no idea. She wishes she could turn these pictures she dreams into story. Into memory. To animate and populate them.

There is one picture that doesn't fit the others – a metal sink, almost a washtub, she thinks in a kitchen, though she has no reason to know this, except maybe for the faucet that rises up a foot or so from the top of the sink before curving gently in an arc like the neck of a swan.

These pictures are significant to Ellen because she is convinced they are images of her childhood. Her earliest verifiable memory is from when she was eight, and even then the age is a guess. The memory is quite different from the pictures she dreams. The memory is of a boardwalk on a beach in Hyannis, on Cape Cod, in summer. Her walking on the sun-bleached wood, sand reflecting heat up at her, her pacing outside a cottage the color of key lime pie. Sometimes in the memory her sister is playing wiffle ball on the other side of the boardwalk, the side away from the house, with a group of children older than Ellen, older like her sister, and Ellen can hear the slap of plastic on plastic as the ball is hit. Sometimes there are sounds of conversation coming from inside the cottage, and Ellen paces the boardwalk, holding her arms out like a tightrope walker, and lets the sounds of wordless voices float into her ears, accompaniment. She also remem-

bers doughnuts, the freshest doughnuts she has ever tasted, doughnuts she would buy from the Costas' market. Now, as an adult, she
realizes the doughnuts were greasy, and that's what made them taste
so good, but she still wishes she could conjure them back: the outside
just the slightest bit crunchy, the inside soft, and still warm.

Warm is safe, safe is the cab of her truck, and these memory-
images are one of the ways she passes the time as she drives. They
are slides reflected on the transparent screen of her windshield. She
doesn't tell Bernie about these. These are a separate set, like the tapes
she makes, or the CB. These are the non-intersecting portions of the
circles of her life. But now there is a baby. There is an inability to
remember the now. There is a chill in the cab, although the fan is
now on 3 and the temperature, Ellen knows, is definitely red. There
is a pull toward the images of the past. Toward dream. Away from
the cab of her truck. Away from the trailer which presses behind her,
the momentum of twenty-two tons of pecans.

She tries the radio again. Is greeted with *PIIGGGGGZOT*. A
sound like a cornered animal. It hurts her ears. She cannot make out
the word baby. Cannot make out any words. Cannot take the assault
on her ears. Cannot be sure she remembers hearing the report.

Even if it is a memory. Even if she did hear it on the radio, how
could she be sure of what she heard. Given the state of the radio. Giv-
en the nature of Ellen. The combination renders certainty unlikely.
But the picture is locked in Ellen's mind. It rests there, clear. Sharp.
A defined image. Given the infrequent nature of these in Ellen's
world, it must be taken seriously. It must be given weight. Substance.
Like the pecans in her trailer. She would like to look at the pecans, to
open the doors of the trailer and let the reality of them anchor her.
But of course she can't. If she were to open the doors, the stampede
would bury her.

There are other reasons why Ellen likes Bernie. His schedule, and the fact he reminds her of her cat. And this: "I've got to keep telling myself the story of who I am in order to get through the day."

Bernie said this the night they were at the Border Cafe, as he made his way through the bean and cheese end of the plate of nachos. Bernie was talking about how strange it is, how disorienting, to work in an office with one-way glass, to know he can see the world, but the world cannot see him. To work at a computer screen programming nearly unfathomable amounts of information onto a piece of plastic and metal the size of a vitamin.

Ellen has seen pictures in her head before. She carries her memory images with her. Sometimes they press themselves upon her, as if they want to tell her things. And she wants to hear those things. She would like to know the things they have to tell her. But always when she listens, the pictures don't speak. They don't take her anywhere. There has never been a baby before. There has never been voice. The memory of voice. The presence of a human. This is why Ellen is listening. This is why Ellen is driving, fast. This is why Ellen has scanned the radio, continues to scan the radio, and curse her broken CB. This is also, she fears, the reason she is suddenly vulnerable to sleep. Suddenly not in control of her sleep. There is a connection. The circles overlap.

"Here's something," Ellen says into her tape recorder. "A black hole warps the geometry of space around it. What does this mean? Gravity is not really a force, but a distortion of space and time. Interesting."

Ellen talks more into the tape recorder now that her CB is broken. She must get it fixed. In the meantime.

"So. The greater the density of an object, the greater its gravitational pull, and the greater the time-space distortion it causes. When the matter in the core of a collapsed star becomes dense enough, space is strongly bent in its vicinity." The cab bounces gently as it moves along the highway. This is one of Ellen's favorite things about driving. "The black hole will swallow up smaller stars near it, hungry to increase its own mass."

Ellen is saying she does not wish to be swallowed up. Bernie will understand this. It is part of their communication system. One of the beautiful things about language.

Here's how it works when Ellen comes unmoored. She will be talking, or thinking, or doing her laundry, and then she will be gone. Later, her eyes will open and she will see the thing that is right in front of her, and then slowly the other things around it, until a vast, wide angle picture comes into view and Ellen's mind registers that she has been gone.

The road signs in New York, on the highways in New York, are green with white lettering. The mile markers are green with white lettering at whole miles, then smaller white signs with black lettering for tenths. When Ellen is particularly bored, or desperately trying to stay awake, she will make up little math problems with the mile markers. Divide the numbers. Two-sixty-one divided by eight. She will calculate it in her head, she will try to finish before she reaches the next marker. It is a way of staying awake.

Ellen is afraid she is going to fall asleep driving. She imagines the load of pecans hurtling down the road, the momentum of forty-four thousand pounds of pecans hurtling along the highway. She imagines the impact, what it would do to her cab. To her. Imagining this helps her to stay awake.

Ellen has decided the baby's name is Bernie. Simplifies things. Everything will be called Bernie today. Baby Bernie is wrapped in a thick white blanket and tucked into a wicker basket. Under the blanket, he wears – or is placed in – a fleece bag with arms, a bag that zips, a bag that covers all of him except his face and his hands. This is the picture in Ellen's mind. There are blue mittens on his hands. There is a picture in Ellen's mind that this is all a picture in Ellen's mind.

Whenever Ellen thinks about snow, she thinks about Vermont. And whenever she thinks about Vermont, she thinks about childhood. She thinks if she were to find this baby, if she had found this baby, if there is a baby, she would take it to Vermont. But the authorities, she can hear Bernie say. You can't do that. But this is only in Ellen's mind, so anything is possible and it is therefore possible Ellen could and would take this baby, Baby Bernie, to Vermont. There are things she believes she could learn from this baby.

Here's what Ellen has learned about the childhood she can't remember: she was adopted young, into the family that vacationed on the Cape, the family that played wiffle ball on the beach. Her parents, the parents she has known, do not know who or where her real parents are. Were prevented from knowing. But Ellen has a family. She is part of a family, and Ellen does not wish to appear ungrateful. Does not wish to *be* ungrateful. It's just that Ellen cannot forget there are two circles – the circle of her life, and the circle of the family she has, the only family she has known – and those two circles are not concentric. There is an overhanging area whose dimensions are not known. Whose substance cannot be known.

Ellen is driving. Her hands tight on the wheel. Her mind on a baby. Wheels rolling beneath her. Pecans rattling in her trailer. Eyes foggy.

She flicks the CB on and then off, on and off, but there is no sound. Not even a hint of static. She wants to piece this together, not to have it fragment even further.

She will keep her eyes open.

She will take pecans to Montreal.

She will pick up a load there, capacitors, a regular load for an electronics company.

She will spend a couple of nights at her apartment. Have dinner with Bernie, wish he could make events stop spinning, and at the same time be glad her life is what it is. That she takes care of herself, can take care of herself. That her mass is not shrinking. That she is not an event horizon.

There is, of course, another possibility, an obvious possibility, which had not occurred to Ellen until now, at mile marker 283 on the New York State Thruway. The baby, of course, could be a girl, a girl named Ellen. This unconsidered possibility intensifies the pull inside Ellen, toward a dark, unfathomable place. It makes her knuckles cold on the steering wheel. Ellen's fingers grip the wheel. Ellen's eyes concentrate on the road. Ellen's mind turns to math problems. Two-sixty-seven times three.

Memory is something Ellen and Bernie discuss a lot. Something she has little of and that surrounds him. Ellen finds it funny that Bernie is able to do this, that there is a whole world able to do this, people who buy memory so they can make use of what Bernie creates.

Memory is a complicated subject for Ellen. "I'd like to be able to remember," she said to Bernie the friend one night in her apartment, while Bernie the cat lapped milk in the kitchen. "But what if it's sealed off for a reason?"

Bernie is not convinced that memory is always a good thing. "Some doors," he said, "should remain closed." Bernie has things he wishes he could forget. Things he tries to forget. That's one of the reasons he likes to work sealed off, in his little room above the highway. "We're built to handle only so much."

Much of what Ellen has read about black holes has stayed with her. She records what she can remember. She concentrates on keeping her eyes open. She pushes the record and play buttons.

"Just as no force in the universe can prevent the forward march of time from past to future outside a black hole, no force in the universe can prevent the inward march of space inside a black hole. Space and time at the center are all jumbled up. They do not exist as separate, distinctive entities." She feels the pull of sleep, and this other pull, toward this baby, toward the radio, toward something that might be memory. "This confusion has profound implications for what goes on inside a black hole. Without a clear, distinct background of space and time, we cannot speak rationally about the arrangement of objects or the ordering of events. Fortunately, we are shielded by the event horizon, so the universe remains understandable and predictable."

A snow squall blows across the road, like a ghost. Jostles the cab. Jostles Ellen alert. She would like to stay awake. She would like to know if there is a baby, and if the baby is Ellen. She is old enough to know we don't get everything we want.

"There exists in the whole quantum theory no cause preventing the system from collapsing into a single point," she says into the microphone.

Ellen has a paycheck in her pocket. Ellen has pecans in her truck. Ellen has a CB radio which is broken. Ellen has a burning in her head, the picture of a baby in a basket. The sound of water. Ellen is thinking strange thoughts. She is thinking she wants to do something for this baby that she isn't sure even exists. That she has no way to locate if it does exist. She needs her CB. She needs to get oriented. "Bernie," she says into her tape recorder. "Bernie I'm about to do a strange thing."

"Consider an astronaut who orbits close to the event horizon. He has a choice: turn around and be saved, or explore closer and be lost to the outside universe forever."

164

Wind whips snow across asphalt. Ellen feels the effort of forcing her eyes open. She considers the possibilities. If there is a baby, and she wants there to be a baby, and for the baby to be Ellen, who would know about it? She is near Glens Falls. Which is near Hudson Falls. There will be a police station. There will be a diner, where there will be news of the baby. Where there will be information.

"Once inside the horizon, it is impossible to prevent the increasingly rapid plunge toward the center of the black hole. Eventually the strong gravity would pull limb from limb and atom from atom until the person was an unrecognizable mass of minute particles. Everything falling into a black hole loses its identity."

Into the tape recorder, Ellen tells how she thinks there is a baby, how there is definitely a paycheck, how there is a diner, where there will be news, and there is a bank, where there will be cash. She thinks about intersecting portions of circles. Shaded areas. A field of virgin snow. Unbroken.

Ellen's eyes see road. Her eyes watch the broken white line that separates one lane from another. Her brain registers an awareness that for some brief time, some unmeasurable moment, Ellen's eyes were not on the road. Were not open. Ellen's foot is on the accelerator. Ellen's fingers are cold. Twenty-two tons of pecans rattling behind her.
"What is the mass of memory, and what can swallow it up?" She says into the tape recorder.
She thinks about remembering. About how she has built a life for herself. About how some parts of circles cannot – should not – overlap. About how some doors should remain closed. She pulls the truck over, onto the shoulder, and stops. She takes a deep breath. She knows that she is lucky. That she cannot count on continuing to be lucky.

She decides there is a baby, and his name is Bernie. She decides some money, her paycheck, will help this baby, Baby Bernie, get a start with his adopted family. She decides that's all she can do.

"Bernie, I did a strange thing today. I'm about to do a strange thing."

A truck passes by. Shaking her. Sending swirls of fine snow dancing in the air above the pavement. Although she is afraid, Ellen gets back on the road. She hangs on, for three miles, until the Peekskill rest stop, where she pulls the truck over, and writes herself a reminder on a Post-It note before yielding to sleep.

terror/home

1.

A SUICIDE BOMBER WITH Hepatitis B, a member of the terrorist wing of Hamas, the fundamentalist Palestinian group, blew himself up in the middle of a crowd of teenage girls outside a disco in Tel Aviv. Killed 22 people. Picture it. As blood and body parts rain down, how many of the survivors were infected. And did he think about that beforehand, this boy: was that part of his satisfaction; his offering.

2.

Beth called. She's in Tucson. Went there to do a conference, now she's stuck. Logan shut down by the storm. Day before yesterday, instead of flying home, she went hiking in Saguaro National Monument. I'm trying to be gracious about this. I'm the one that loves the desert, plus I'm not good when she's away.

"Come home," I plead.

"Soon as I can get a flight," she says.

"Fly somewhere close and take a bus. A train. Walk."

"Take a breath. Have some soup. Do laundry. I'll be there when I can."

3.

It started snowing on Tuesday and hasn't stopped. Twenty-four inches the first 24 hours. Now eighty-two, and counting. I'm hunkered down in the kitchen with my tea and my radio and my laptop and my dog, Blue. I've dragged a sled to the corner store to stock up on soup and bread, oatmeal and bananas. I've shoveled the walk, twice, then surrendered. Let it come.

"The paper began falling in Carroll Gardens Brooklyn after the second plane hit on that Tuesday morning," the radio guy says. "At St. Paul's Cemetery in Manhattan, three inches of paper blanketed the graves."

I want someone's warm breath on my face.

4.

Start here. Allison and I in kayaks on the Swift River. It's an autumn afternoon and we've been talking and drinking dark beer in Allison's kitchen and now we're out on the river in kayaks with the sun ducking in and out of clouds and the air cold enough that we're aware of it, and appreciative of the sun. We decided to go the other direction than we usually go: toward the waterfall. We'd both known of it, but never seen it (this was in the early days, when Allison first lived in Belchertown). We trusted we'd see it before the current drew us too close. I remember downed tree limbs poking up from the water, the smooth decay of it all. Us in wood chairs by the wood stove before, with the window open a crack and Allison smoking and us talking about how she was going to stop drinking next month, and then deciding to drag out the kayaks. The exhilarating breath of friendship. The silly, adolescent deliciousness of going close to the waterfall, of finding the edge and dancing there.

5.

Winter has come on in a hurry. I thought I would resist it, that the transition would take a long, grudging time. Instead, a three-day wind came through, blew away what leaves remained, and left winter in its wake. I watched the leaves turn, swirl slowly to the ground, clusters of them blown down my narrow street like small armadas. Watched them lose their last bit of life on the dogwood out front, until they dangled dead, fodder for the wind which seemed ordained. All things being equal, I'd prefer 70 and sunny, but there'll be a season again for that. Now is the time for hibernation.

The act with value for me is the archaeological. My job is to sift through the rubble to see what remains.

the angel dreams of home. she wears a green jumpsuit and a black baseball cap with cloth wings stitched to the side, the wings stuffed with bits of cotton so they puff out, cartoonish. she is weary, weakened. now bandaging the wounded in a Tel Aviv pizzeria, now hauling debris from the World Trade Center site. in the first days, she'd go to Washington Square Park and read remembrances. sit with those who waited for news of loved ones. she daily trades cold for fatigue, the one flowing to the other within the first hour, the process familiar, ache to ache. she works 70 feet below street level in a massive bathtub half-filled with dirt and twisted metal.

she wears thick rubber gloves and a mask. the hat she bought at penn station. she removes soggy slop, little of it identifiable. she has a union dock worker's card, and the skills to back it up. she eats a cheese sandwich and an orange and watches people watch the recovery work. every fifth or sixth person wearing one of those paper masks to filter out bad air. there's a heavyset man in a blue suit who holds a handkerchief in front of his mouth and nose. she wonders whether he has forgotten his mask, or does not wish to acknowledge the need. she has seen him here before.

she wears out three or four pairs of gloves every day. she works alongside many of the same people, but they rarely talk. they dig through metal, mud and plaster, twisted steel and charred wood. they straddle the slurry, buckets in hand, looking for even a hint of human remains. she watches

the trucks cart it all away and thinks about what else those trucks will
carry to staten island. what will be borne there.
    she craves steamed clams at the ocean. she sets herself practical tasks
in the evenings. she re-wires a lamp. refinishes a small bookcase.

6.

    Allison needs to check herself into detox. But this is the down
side of being broke in Belchertown. The prospects are grim. A humorless lock-up, and AA meetings in the basement of some small-
town church that always smells of wet plaster. She's still sorting out
what happened in California, the aftershocks of betrayal, the accep-
tance of living on disability though she's physically fit. As idyllic and
quiet as it is in their little house on the Swift River, it is also isolated.
A sea change from L.A. And her pit bull Ingrid is having a series of
run-ins with a porcupine. Quilled twice while on nightly walkabout.
The vet met them in the emergency room; he removed more than
two hundred quills.

    "They've got little hooks on the end of them, so you can't just
pull them out." It took nearly three hours, Allison told me. "She
looked like a pin cushion." The last time Allison was in detox, she
was at McLean, with Joan Kennedy, who arrived wearing one leop-
ard-skin boot. We've spent a lot of time in front of the wood stove,
Allison and Ingrid and I.

    "You gotta keep her away from that porcupine." Ingrid is a sweet
dog. She stands on her hind legs and head butts me every time I come
in.

    "It's how she's built," Allison says. "Either she gets the porcupine,
or the porcupine gets her."

7.

    Here's what I love about Beth: she can't get warm. Spends each
winter seeking thicker or more effective layers. Combs catalogs for
clothing advancements. New fabrics. Improved, interlocking fleeces.

I like winter, how she needs me for heat, cozies up to me in bed. She worries that I forget the practical things. I get involved in projects and forget to eat. To store in enough wood for the stove when she's away. And this: sometimes in bed, her head on my chest, conversation faded, I'm lost in restfulness, then I feel her tense, and lift her head, her eyes on mine, and say, softly, "Breathe."

8.

And then this: Aqraba, outside Nablus, on the West Bank, olive groves. Trees whose harvest has fed families for generations. Whose yield is a crucial part of sustenance. Okay, then. An October morning. Dozens of Palestinians walk toward their trees. Families, friends. Harvest time. They make the walk at this time every year, early morning, before the sun bakes the day, over the crest of a hill, across a swath of stones, along a dirt road. Men and boys, women and girls.

Don't make it idyllic. It's not. The boys complain about the work to come, reflex more than resistance. They'd rather watch television. Their friends will soon gather for football. One boy stumbles on a rock. His cohorts laugh. Ahead, behind wrought iron, the Itamar settlement runs the length of the neighboring hilltop. On the hill, a handful of settlers with rifles. The day before, they'd surrounded the group. Rifle butts into ribs. Intimidation. Today, they stand on the hill and watch. Then there are shots. First, into the air. People scatter. Many scramble back up the hill toward home. Then one falls, and another. A 24-year-old shot dead, in the back, as he turns for home.

Later, one settler, handgun on hip, interviewed for American radio. "Of course there are olive farmers," he said. "And there are terrorists." He cocked his head against the midday sun. "Can *you* tell the difference?"

9.

Allison called today. She's teaching a class of business majors, as part of a joint program between the School of Management and the

English Department. The management professor designs the assignments; the English professor works on the writing. This week, the students have written explosions memos. Letters to their mythical CEOs containing recommendations about how to handle corporate communications when a disgruntled employee attempts to blow up the building. Allison called to tell me Ingrid got the porcupine. "I found it dead, belly up outside the front door," she said. "I have no idea how she managed it." Allison went to an AA meeting last night, in Amherst. "It was okay. Some of the people had a sense of humor."

she is a student of numbers, fascinated by the scope of them, the implications – 108,444 truckloads of debris, 1,642,698 tons of rubble, 190,568 tons of steel. 19,559 body parts. the debris is taken to Fresh Kills, a re-opened landfill on Staten Island, where it is searched by police and public health officials, every bucket still sifted for body parts. a search dog with human crew picks through a spot where a revolving door exit once led to Liberty Street. a grappler digs a careful trench from the west side of the foundation toward the center. one small load at a time. she is not the last person to handle the slop. new york city medical examiners work to match DNA samples with bits of flesh, some small as a finger. at first, she worked on sheer adrenaline, in complete confusion. fires burned. volunteers poked through piles of slurry. she re-learned how quickly emotion gives way to exhaustion. to work by force of will, sheer purpose. she has a sore back, the muscles tight near her tailbone, so she stretches every morning before work.

10.

Warm breath on my face. It's 6:30 am and the dog wants to go out. I once wanted to build gleaming structures, scale mountains. Achievement and recognition. These days I walk through the ruins of that dream. And I discipline myself to look around. I told Beth about this one winter night, huddled close. She asked, "What do you recognize in the ruins?" And I had to think for a minute, to conjure the picture in my head before I could answer: "Human faces."

We're all escaping something, Beth says. The question is what are we escaping from, and what are we escaping to. I marvel at her. I swore she was on the verge of sleep, and she comes out with this. She has these moments.

"Tell me more, " I say. But she shrugs. She feels no need to put it all together.

I know, I know: the dog.

11.

The radio guy says the government's official report on the events of September 11 is so huge that the two dozen staff investigators will not be able to read it in their lifetime.

Beth called. Logan still closed. She's considering flights to Hartford, even New York, where it's turned to rain. "Listen," I tell her. I've been thinking about the struggle to retain meaning in life. "Commercials are intimate, and better scripted. What does that leave us?"

Silence, then: "Have you spoken with anyone today?"

"Yes." I can hear defensiveness in my voice. "Richard, the guy at the corner store. We talked about economics. He taught me about the various uses of capital. Drew it out for me on a paper bag."

"Call someone," she says. "Go for coffee."

"It's a blizzard," I remind her. "I had to fight just to open the door."

Beth takes these trips, a week at a time – Des Moines, Toronto, Omaha. Talks to groups about business systems. They're middle managers, mostly, trying to better organize departments, reduce budgets. Conscientious folks. I tell her she's lucky she's so extroverted. "This isn't natural to me," she says. "You know better than that." She's right. She's worked at it, because this work is what she can do. I've become more insular. Dangerously so, according to Beth. "You need to put yourself out there," she says. "What are you waiting for?"

12.

The Asian brown gas cloud, a two-mile thick blanket of pollution over south Asia, may be causing the premature deaths of a half million people in India each year. According to a UN-sponsored study, it contributes to deadly flooding in some areas and drought in others. "The grimy cocktail of ash, soot, acids and other damaging airborne particles is as much the result of wood and dung-burning stoves, cookfires and forest clearing as it is of industry."

13.

Couldn't sleep. Watched part of an old prison movie on TV. William Holden. Toward the end he tells someone (girlfriend?), "I'm not sure I can make it on the outside." I know how he feels. Susan's on the West Bank, riding in ambulances back and forth from Nablus to the hospitals across guarded roads, because her presence as an American makes it less likely the ambulances will be detained at checkpoints. Every day, she's in the face of Israeli soldiers. Carla's fighting cancer. I keep fighting the desire to be someone I'm not. To lead the cavalry as they ride in to save the day. Beth keeps encouraging me: do what's in front of you.

home is a studio apartment on the lower east side. the shower folds out from the kitchen sink. a sofa folds out as the bed. a storage drawer underneath holds the objects she treasures here, now: an unopened package of drake's yodels, intact somehow in the ruins; a mouse from a macintosh, sleek plastic surface inviting fingers.

the weight of wet drywall depresses her; the volume and the slop of it; the waste. it's this she tires of moving, of seeing. the unexpected heft of plaster and paper, the unrelenting volume, the festering wet.
in the beginning, she would go home at night and repair things, soak her feet in warm water and watch the final minutes of the knicks game on a reclaimed 14-inch television. now she spends nearly all her time at the

site. twelve-hour shifts, sometimes fourteen, then she'll find a spot, out of the way, to watch. when the february cold conquers her, a walk to the construction trailer for coffee, a honey-dipped doughnut.

she was in a tel aviv open-air pizzeria, wiping spattered blood off greasy walls. she can always feel it coming, when she'll be relocated. sadness overtakes her. the earth becomes an ocean liner, engines reversing. she scrubbed harder, one of those abrasive sponges, her strong arms, to erase even the shadow of the stain. the force of the blast picked her off her feet, blew her here. she will never, could never, anaesthetize herself from the impact, but she has disciplined herself to let it pass, to lose herself in the moment of travel. there is comfort, even a guilty pleasure, in being carried this way. a rush of joy in the paradoxical freedom.

now she sits on the trailer steps, warms her hands around a paper cup of steaming coffee in the lonely hours before dawn and watches the work below. the hydraulic brake line on a grappler bursts, arcing fluid over a crew working to reinforce the bathtub's eastern retaining wall; steel tie-back cables threaded through the surface to bedrock. the grappler operator shuts the machine down. a man joins her at the trailer steps, warming his gloves on the exhaust from the generator.

"we're getting close," she says. "not much longer."

he rubs his hands together. "tell you a secret," he says. "i'm scared."

they talk without looking at one another. they watch the fluid-spattered work crew secure cables.

"how's that?" she asks.

"long as I keep at it," the man says, "i'm too tired to feel. at some point, there'll be hell to pay."

14.

Here's how Allison is built. She drove up - materialized, more like, in a 1963 Studebaker, aqua and cream. The windows rolled down, her arm out, as if it were summer. "Hop in," she said. That grin of hers. "Let's go for a ride." I was out in the yard, raking leaves. On a new kick to exercise discipline. A three-day wind had stripped the trees bare, and I'd been to the hardware store to buy some of those paper yard waste bags.

I didn't know where she got the car. I didn't ask, and she didn't tell, until we had picked up Carla and Susan and were halfway to New York. I just put the rake away, changed jackets, and hopped in.

She passed me a flask filled with good tequila, and I drank some. "I've been depressed about this for a week," she said. "I had to *do* something."

Susan came along as if she'd known this was happening. Carla we had to work on a bit. "You need to do this," Allison said. Carla stood in her driveway, arms crossed against the chill. Smiling. It mattered that we'd come. She'd been diagnosed with Hodgkin's. A tumor the size of an orange, next to her heart.

"Where are we going?"

"I don't know. We'll have you back in 24 hours. We'll make sure you get rest."

We ended up at a club in Soho listening to the Kinsey Report, a Chicago blues band that's a favorite of Carla's. We just walked by the place and saw their name on a chalkboard in the window. That's how it is with Allison sometimes. Then we wandered through Chelsea talking, and ended up at a pool hall where Allison won a hundred dollars playing eight ball for ten bucks a game. I don't even remember how that started – a joke somehow about her erratic play. Then we were lining up challengers. She couldn't lose. We got a hotel room. Susan and I crashed on the floor, gave Carla and Allison the bed. Rode home in the morning, in the Studebaker, which belonged to Ben's boss. Allison's son Ben is a cinematographer – these days he shoots mostly rap videos – she convinced him to loan her the car. Wide bench seats. Crisp autumn air through the windows. We felt like royalty. Had Carla back in 24 hours, Allison true to her word. She can't abide feeling stuck. Standing still.

Now Carla's cancer free, and while I'm not crazy enough to claim a direct relationship, I think Allison matters.

15.

Carla visualizes angels massaging her chest, her heart. Kneading her until the tumor, once swollen, first shrinks, then slides away. Her faith and quiet determination are a marvel to me. "What do these angels look like?"

"I don't envision their faces – only their hands. They have strong hands. You can see the muscles flex as they work. One of them bites her nails. Her touch is fast and restless. The other slow and deep. Hers are a runner's hands."

"What do a runner's hands look like?"

Carla looks at her own hands. Holds them up before me. "You can just tell. Hands are hard to describe."

16.

More than 200 Tibetan exiles stormed the Chinese embassy in Kathmandu. Police beat them back with bamboo batons. At least 130 were arrested, and one foreigner saw four refugees beaten so badly that police sprinkled white powder on the ground to cover the blood.

17.

"I've got a flight." Beth's voice on the phone. The dog and I watch snow out the kitchen window. It's got a hypnotic effect. I couldn't say how long we've been sitting here. "Direct into Newark."

We're up over four days, a hundred hours, and it has slowed but not stopped. Thicker flakes and slow. History will keep coming back until we get the story straight. So we're left here with ourselves and the snow. "Thanks."

"There's only so much you can do in Tucson."

"I'll shovel the walk."

"Still coming down, huh? It must be beautiful."

"Mesmerizing." I picture her journey, creating in my head one of those old-movie maps that traces a dotted line as you travel. Flight to Newark, bus to New York, then the train. We'll meet her at the subway, Blue and I and the sled, and pull her home.

Last Seen, Hank's Grille

WHAT CAN I TELL YOU? Only what I have seen. What I have pieced together from the reports of others, and filtered by my own experience. Perceptions which are inadequate and inconclusive. Theories and abstractions about a damaged world, when what everyone wants from me – a witness – is a coherent version of events.

I throw up my hands, befuddled. You will want to punch me. It's happened already. My snout broken and bloodied for no reason other than I spoke the truth. That I cannot say with any certainty what happened out there.

Becca says that's bullshit. Maybe she's right.

All I know is her brother is missing, and she blames me.

Becca has theories of her own. She is of the opinion that Tom has a head injury, that this explains his decreasing interest in things like paying his bills on time, or his willingness to drive cross-country with Fillmore Priest. Although I don't believe it's true, her theory is more plausible than you might think. Tom talked about a fall he took in February, shortly after he moved to Massachusetts, to Ashland. How his front walkway was coated in black ice. How his feet went out from under him and he flew, a tangle of arms and legs, landing ass over teakettle on the walk. He laughed about it later, his introduction to the east coast after nearly a decade in Texas. A concussion, a few hours of jumbled memories, maybe an increased sense of forgetfulness. And while he hasn't had any physical problems since, Becca believes something happened there. That Tom maybe cracked his head on the stone step and the delicate mystery that is the human brain was affected.

Of course, Becca also believes it's my fault that Tom is homosexual. She's determined not to resent Tom for it. Says she's trying to hate the sin, but love the sinner. I want to ask her how she feels about that now, with Tom missing, but my nose is too sore to get hit again.

Becca is a believer. She is able to view the world in discernible shapes and patterns, to form an opinion and stick to it. I've never been able to see things that clearly. The way I see it, none of us humans is intact. We carry a besieged past, inhabit a confused present. What beliefs and values we do pass on are increasingly inadequate to account for the world around us. I believe that the ability to believe has been compromised, maybe irreparably, and that we live in an age where apostasy is necessary: a means of survival, maybe even a source of enlightenment.

This is the shit that drives Becca crazy.

Tom is brilliant. Though it took him a while to find something he wanted to apply himself to. He worked for the Peace Corps in Indonesia. Got a law degree and stumbled into a job as in-house counsel for a biotech firm. Couple years later went to medical school then transferred to study genetics. He looks like a scientist. Thin, intense, a little aloof. That thing with his eyes where even when he's looking right at you, he's looking beyond you. Anyway, he became fascinated by research he'd read on human aging, and the possibility that it could be arrested. It was all about understanding disease in a new way, he said, and using genetics to find treatments. None of us thought Tom would last, but he did; earned his doctorate in cell biology from the Baylor School of Medicine, and caught on with a team working to isolate the aging gene. It's not as crazy as it sounds. A telomere is a cap at the end of a DNA string, which shortens every time a cell divides. When the cap is used up, the DNA is exposed and the cell dies. But if these telomeres could be lengthened, the cell could live longer. Maybe a lot longer. There were scientists who believed in the existence of a telomerase gene, and in the '90s, they found the scientific climate to support them. Funding for their projects. Publicity. Enthusiasm. Tom was one of those scientists. And Fillmore Priest is where he found his money.

"The facts, Max," Becca says to me. "Just the fucking facts."
Becca never says fuck. Her knuckles are still swollen from where she broke my nose. I take perverse satisfaction in my ability to annoy her.
Okay, the facts. Tom and Fillmore Priest and I rented a 1976 Cadillac El Dorado convertible, filled a cooler with ice and Coronas and Priest's baby-shit-brown blend of wheatgrass and carrot juice, and hit the highway. Destination: Nogales Mexico, a little restaurant called the Las Vegas Café that has the best *ropas vieja* that any of us has ever tasted. Crazy as Priest is, I do enjoy his company. And when he and Tom get going, even if two-thirds of what they say sails straight over my head, it makes me smile. It's inspiring. Although I will never taste greatness myself, I do like to be near it, and greatness seems to enjoy my underachieving company. But I digress. Two days into our road trip, near a truck stop outside of Abilene where we'd stopped in search of chili dogs, Tom wandered off. Disappeared. And, although it makes no logical sense when you consider the circumstances, I don't think Tom is missing. I think he left.

I've met some odd characters over the years, but none odder than Fillmore Priest, a geophysicist who'd made his fortune finding oil. Could sniff it out like a dog. Priest, now in his seventies, has devoted his later years to a single goal: he wants to be the first person to live to

200. "Hell," he told me the first time I met him. "We should be able to do as good as turtles."

I'd gone to visit Tom in Houston in 1995, during the start of his third year at Baylor. He had a work dinner, and wanted me to come along. The guy he was meeting was a character; I would love him.

That night Tom and Priest and I ate steaks and Gulf shrimp and drank martinis, and I first heard Priest's wild thoughts about the "cure" for old age. Priest barely fit at the table – he's an enormous man with a bald skull and a delicate face. Soft skin still tinged baby pink, and damn near wrinkle-free.

"I'm having an extremely happy life," he told me, a bubble of steak sauce hanging on his lip. "Why should I have to die."

Tom raised his eyebrows at me, and ate. He was always hungry then – you couldn't fill him up.

"I have more money than God," Priest said, in a gruff voice too loud for the half-full restaurant. "And yet every year, I grow more terrified of death."

It was one of those places with a cigar room, all brass sconces and mahogany, the musk of serious business deals in the air. Priest leaned toward me; his green eyes, framed behind magnifying glass lenses, bored into mine. Our dinner plates were massive. "Do you know how many vitamin pills I take every day?"

I shook my head, "No, sir."

He wore a coral-colored golf shirt nearly the same tint as his skin. There was muscle in his bulk. There seemed no way he could be in his seventies. "Guess."

Tom watched us, intent, his fork in steady rhythm, plate to mouth to plate. Shrimp. Steak. Shrimp.

I shrugged. "Six?"

"Fifty-five." Each syllable punctuated with a poke of his index finger on the table. "Fifty-five god damned vitamins every day. A regimen of karate. And I can't shake the terror of dying. What do you think of that?"

All I could think of was the sight of this enormous perspiring man bowing in a white robe.

"Fillmore has formed a society," Tom said. His angular frame did not fit well in chairs. "The Cure Old Age Right Now God Dammit Society." He cut a piece of steak. Let it absorb the juices. Chewed bread as he spoke. "If you're not careful, Max, he'll recruit you."

"He mocks me." Priest spoke to me, convivial "But we're a team. Joined on a common quest. Because I've given your friend and his cohorts more than a million dollars to make a start."

I concentrated on my meal, eating shrimp to hide my chagrin. I'd never thought about the scads of money that must lie behind serious scientific research. I didn't want to. I wanted only to think of pristine laboratories far from the demands of commerce.

Priest held his fork aloft. "Most of the world suffers from occluded vision," he said. "The inability to see beyond the end of their noses. Tom's gift is he's willing to go into uncharted territory." Priest wrapped an arm around Tom . "He's a visionary, like me."

Tom put his own arm around Priest's shoulder. The pair of them, intertwined like ceramic monkeys. Tom's face wore a mix of pride and something else. The expression stuck in my mind and later, on the way back to his apartment, I identified it as mischief. Like a child who's getting away with something in plain sight of the adults.

"You don't buy that stuff?" I asked him. "I mean, there's no science there."

It was a warm night in Houston. We wore short sleeve shirts and the flush of good alcohol. Though nearly a head taller than me, Tom slouched when he drank, diminishing the distance between us. He was quiet a minute before answering. "Priest's money can put him at the forefront of scientific development. He's engaged with smart people, exciting work, and that makes him feel alive."

"Sure, he's a good way to get funding." Deep night. The streets were deserted. The city ours.

"In science, the questions we start out asking aren't always the ones that get answered. They may become the engine that drives the work toward some related end." Only when Tom saw my puzzled face did he say more. "We could be two or three years from a breakthrough, Max. Think about that." His eyes doing that thing they do. "To me, this is a religious question. I want to work to end human suffering. Behind suffering is disease, and behind disease is aging."

That was the only answer I ever got. I spent that night – and a good part of the next several weeks – thinking about it all. I decided I was proud of my friend's resourcefulness. How he was able to steer a rich old man's delusions toward enriching human life.

Tom's situation reminds me of Katie, a woman I knew for a time after college. A bunch of us were working for a market research firm in Brooklyn. Everyone there had something else they "really" did – poets, playwrights, painters – but Katie was maybe the most eclectic of us all. She drifted through her days, trying out everything, tying herself to nothing, and this free-floating quality was essential to her being. Her respiratory system. Two or three guys and as many women got seriously hung up on her, pressed her for constancy. But that wasn't how Katie worked. She was with who she was with for today; tomorrow it might all be different.

We drove to Minneapolis one night on a whim, Katie and Judy and Lori and I, and somewhere in Wisconsin, or maybe Iowa, a few wild horses ran up beside the road, running full tilt, nostrils flaring in the moonlight. They must have run with us for close to a mile. None of us saw where they came from, but while we watched them Katie told me about growing up, how she'd never go back to the places she had already lived – Chicago, San Diego, Eugene. That when she left a place, she left it for good. Friends and all. People think big change only happens through some cataclysmic event, some traceable root cause. But Katie just slipped out the back door.

We headed south through D.C., Virginia. Then on into Kentucky, Missouri, Arkansas. Our own erratic route to Mexico. I hadn't seen Priest in a couple years, and he was all giddy banter before we settled into the drowsy, quiet rhythm of a long ride. Tom was subdued. His eyes tired. He and I shared the driving.

Outside Bowling Green. Rolling pasture. Herefords grazing in afternoon sun. Priest uncorked a quart bottle of his juice concoction. He had eight more packed in dry ice in the trunk. It was all he would consume until Nogales. I winced at the odor.

"Careful with that. Four cows just keeled over."

Tom's beer-lazy voice from the back seat. "Be glad it's a convertible. He starts to reek."

"Laugh if you want," Priest said, brandishing his bottle, "but this has made me what I am today."

I kept a loose grip on the wheel. "A smelly old fuck who's scared of dying?"

Priest feigned a scowl and sipped at the bottle. He wore a white towel on his head, secured with a leather band. Wraparound sunglasses with an extra tinted plastic shield tucked into them that covered all the way around past his temples. "Why'nt you boys let me drive?"

"Because you're old and unsteady," I teased. "Because we want to live."

"My ass." Priest delivered a powerful kendo punch toward the dashboard. "I could kick the shit out of both of you." His face wore that grin that is my gift to him. I can amuse, but I don't invest. When things stop being easy, I stop doing them. By the time I recognized this as a character flaw, it was too deep in me to change.

Tom drove all night. He had an open road, a dogged disposition, and a sky full of stars. "Hand me a beer, Max."

Priest dozed in and out. His lips burbled when he slept, then he'd nag at us, a human No-Doz. "Go easy on the *cerveza*."

Tom watched the road. "Sure thing, boss."

"It's not me I'm thinking of, it's you." Priest leaned against the head rest, spoke toward the back seat. "I've got to take good care of my scientist."

"Fuck you." Tom's face inscrutable in the dashlight.

"He doesn't like it when I get proprietary," Priest said.

"He doesn't like it when you talk about him in the third person," Tom said.

I've wondered sometimes if the two of them were lovers, if that's part of what drew them together. But Tom has long lived like a monk, singularly devoted to his work.

A shadowy tree line interrupted the night sky. Tires hissed beneath us.

"I don't think our friend has ever fully accepted the fact that the real science," Priest raised a finger, "and the publicity – went the other way. Stem cells and all."

Tom adjusted mirrors.

"He and I are the lunatic fringe now." Priest shifted his bulk on the seat. "But he doesn't like that. He wants the big answers and the glory, too. Only it doesn't often work that way."

"We're on vacation." Tom turned up the radio, some generic '70s pop tune. Priest merely raised his own volume to compensate.

"Did you know our boy has a religious background? He keeps thinking he wants to be a functionary. Tidy little experiments to demonstrate obvious truths. But we know better, don't we Max. If that's what he really wanted, he wouldn't have come home to me."

For two years, from autumn 1995 through summer '97, Tom and his team worked at isolating a telomerase gene. I'd never seen him happier. He and Priest and I had dinner a few times, even took our first road trip, heading out through west Texas toward Death Valley. I had been skeptical about the marriage of science and commerce, but both Tom and Priest were confident. Quirky pals with a shared hobby. "It's a great relationship," Tom told me. "Sure, Priest has an eccentric side. But he respects the science." Then, in August of '97, the research team found a telomerase gene. In the process, though, they also found evidence – a lot of evidence, Tom told me – that telomeres were not the whole story on aging. That they didn't know what the rest of the story was, and that even the telomeres part of it could take years to piece together. Tom was inconsolable. But there was more: around the same time, significant work had been done on stem cells, with promising implications for their application to disease treatment. In this, science works like anything else: suddenly the attention, the thinking – and the money that supported the thinking – went into stem cell research. Priest followed the crowd, found a new golden boy. And that was that.

Tom holed up in Houston. From what I could tell, he wasn't even working. Then, last fall, Priest came back into the picture; although the spotlight stayed on stem cell work, Tom moved to Ashland with scads of money, a new lab, and a new sense of purpose. That's when Becca really began to worry.

We'd pulled off Interstate 20 in Abilene, headed south or maybe east on some state road. Tom and I drank Coronas like water, and Priest sipped at his viscous blend of wheatgrass and carrot juice. We don't like the franchise shops you find at the side of the highway. We prefer to dig a little into the land, find home cooking. We were hungry for chili dogs, like I said. And we all had to piss, what with the beer and juice in all that heat. So we bypassed the Stuckey's and followed the two-lane blacktop out past the municipal airport toward Clyde.

We drove unhurried, top down, AM radio playing honest-to-God country music, Priest's bald head covered in a tan cloth hat.

"I can almost taste those dogs," Priest said. "The melted cheese. The congealed grease. The chili seeping into the roll." Not that he would eat one. He'd live vicariously through Tom and I. Bask in the aromas, watch us with the intensity of a hungry pit bull. It was a little off-putting when you first encountered it, him hovering over your food, nose in the air, head dancing sometimes to within inches of your plate, then retreating, a greedy olfactory orbit. But we'd been down this road with Priest before.

"Try not to slobber on Max's shirt this time," Tom called out.

A couple songs down the road, at a convergence of two truck routes, we found nirvana. Hank's Grille. Burgers. Chili dogs. Hank's wasn't simply a roadside café; it was a service complex, maybe the only real accommodation for miles around. Gas station. Convenience store. Whole outbuilding for rest rooms.

We pulled into the hardpack parking lot, kicked up dust. Tom shifted into park and turned off the engine, and we all took a minute to stretch and otherwise accustom ourselves to the absence of motion.

"My head hurts," Priest said. He removed his hat and rubbed his scalp. He had covered himself with sunblock, SPF 60.

We would go in separate directions. Tom to the convenience store for pretzels and jerky and whatever else looked good for snacking. Priest to the outbuilding for the men's room.

"There'll be one in the café," I told him.

He put the hat on. Adjusted his head under it. "I've had nothing but shit juice for 36 hours."

"Right. Take your time. I'll get us a table."

Tom rubbed his eyes. The chili dogs had been his idea.

So we went each to our tasks, expecting to converge in a few minutes. Tom took nothing with him. I sat in the booth – vinyl seats, Formica tabletop – and thumbed through the selections on the individualized juke box, salivating for a chili dog I would never get.

Tom and Becca and I grew up together in the suburbs outside Akron. Their family was religious, mine wasn't, but I went to church with them – Southern Baptist – and half lived at their house through my adolescence. Tom drifted from both his faith and his family in college; for a while, I was about the only one he'd talk to. He wanted to believe, and if you could create faith through sheer effort, Tom would have done it. But I guess he couldn't reconcile the church he knew with the world he saw, with his own emerging inclinations. Because college is also when he came out, and his family struggled with that. Especially Becca. She's told me more than once how Tom chose first homosexuality, and then science, over God; but how she believes he has a firm foundation, and that someday he'll come back.

Becca is sure of herself in ways that Tom never was. Maybe that's what happens when you spend your formative years hiding who you are. So it interests me that Tom chose science in the end, as if he, like Becca, had been searching for a system that could supply answers. Becca has speculated that Tom was daunted by the time it would take to piece together an answer; that he left this work, as he'd left so many other things, when he saw he couldn't make a big impact right away. I'm not denying that's there. Tom had – has – an ego. But I think what discouraged him – if he was discouraged – was the possibility that there were pieces of this puzzle he might never be able to identify. That its boundaries were more expansive than he'd thought, and that therefore he might never *know*.

The waitress brought three waters.

I watched the glasses sweat and thought of Priest fouling the air of the rest room. I fished four quarters from my pocket and picked three songs I didn't know.

Priest came through the door halfway through the second song, a white handkerchief moist on his head, newly clad in a white long-sleeve shirt.

"How could my head get sunburned through a hat?"

I shrugged. "Sun's out. We're in a convertible."

"Through a hat, Max. This is the purpose of hats." He removed the handkerchief. His skull *was* a touch pink. "I could get skin cancer."

"It's just the heat raising your blood." I touched the top of his head. "Doesn't feel like sunburn."

"It's sunburn, god dammit."

I shrugged. "We'll get some aloe vera."

While Buddy Miller sang "Somewhere Trouble Don't Go," Priest grunted and dug a tube of sunblock out of his pack, rubbed some on his head, then carefully replaced the moist handkerchief. "Shut up."

We waited through the end of the song, sipped water and looked over our menus. The air conditioning an elixir.

"Tom must be overwhelmed by the jerky selection."

I moved to find him. Priest followed a minute later.

We made a circuit of the place and wound up back at the car. No sign of Tom. Keys in the ignition.

"What the fuck?" Priest rearranged the handkerchief on his head, pulled the hat gently on over it. We looked around. The guy at the gas pumps – early 20s, already a few exits along the road to nowhere – sat watching us from a folding chair in the shade.

"We've got to do something about this," Priest said. "Tom's been taken." His voice lacked some of its authority. His face some of its color.

"Tom hasn't been *taken*."

"He has."

"How?"

"Abducted by aliens. Kidnapped by fucking Zapatistas. How should I know." He rubbed the back of his neck. Touched the top of his head. "How else do you explain this. Where could he have *gone*?"

He had a point. A hot breeze blew dust at our feet. There were maybe four other cars, a couple rigs parked in the back.

Eerie quiet. Lots of nothing, as far as you could see.

"We must have missed him," I said. "Check the men's room. The women's. Maybe he wandered in by mistake. Dozed off."

"He's fucking gone."

I didn't believe it, not for a while, but of course Priest turned out to be right.

We talked to waitresses. The grill man. The guy pumping gas. The only one who'd noticed Tom was the convenience store clerk. And even then all we learned was that he bought a bottle of water and some jerky. Possibly a granola bar.

"We gather a posse," Priest said. Water in one hand, juice in the other. "Look for roving packs of bandits. Wild dogs. Skate punks." He pulled up one sleeve to his elbow. Felt the skin of his forearm. "Stress is not good for me," he said. "These wrinkles. They weren't here an hour ago."

We drove the area. I climbed to the tops of whatever puny hills we passed. We asked anyone we saw.

Priest stood in the passenger seat, sunglasses surveying the endless empty land. One hand gripped the rim of the windshield, the other his hat. Chin thrust out defiantly at the desert that had swallowed Tom. "What do you know about skinheads," he shouted against the wind. "What are their habits? Where do they gather?"

There was nothing out there. Nowhere to go. As far as anyone at Hank's could remember, no cars or trucks had left between the time we pulled in and the time Tom went missing.

"I gotta take my vitamins." Parked on the shoulder of State Route 36. Priest reached into the back seat for a small duffel he kept just for his pill supply, housed in those plastic dispensers where you can pre-arrange your dosages. He had three installments for each day. He swallowed fifteen, twenty pills with water. The process took a while. He tossed the dispenser back into the duffel, the duffel onto the bench seat.

"What the fuck," he said. Between the hat and the sunglasses, Priest's big face was nearly hidden.

We stopped at the airport. The train station in Abilene. The bus depot. No one had seen Tom, no one remembered. We went to the police, but it's hard for them to get worked up over a healthy adult who wandered off only a few hours before.

"Is he mentally ill? Does he have some physical handicap?" The desk sergeant looked young and spindly, baby face and wire-rimmed glasses. He looked like a high school kid visiting the station on take-your-son-to-work day. He feigned patience with us.

I stood at the desk. Priest muttered and paced behind me on marbled linoleum. "Watch for reports of banditos crossing the border," he said. "A fledgling terrorist group opposed to scientific advancement, fronted by a disenchanted heiress."

The sergeant stared through me at Priest. He looked down at a notepad, then up at me. "As far as you know, did he have a wallet with him? Credit cards? A driver's license?"

I nodded.

Priest had walked to the water fountain; he wet the handkerchief, placed it back on his head. He gestured toward the sergeant. "He's ignoring me. Tell him I hate being ignored."

The desk sergeant kept his eyes on me and shrugged. "People take off." If he gained two hundred pounds, he could be Priest's grandson. The baby face. "We'll monitor the hospitals, see if a body turns up."

"Ask him are there Zapatistas in the area." Priest addressed me. "Are we close to Waco? Are any of those nutballs left alive?" Droplets of water ran down the back of his neck.

Now that Becca knows a little more about Priest, she thinks he's certifiable. And I can't explain the fact that he and I are friends. Why I find myself defending him to Becca; why I try to make the case that he is at heart a good man, even a religious man. She gets that look in her eyes and raises her index finger at me. "Satan is a religious man," she says. And I know what she means. There may be something ruthless about the way Priest has used Tom's ambition. But that cuts both ways.

We spent the night at the Derrick Motel in Clyde, Texas. Checked in with the police the next morning. Drove two-lane roads all day until our vision blurred. Hounded the police again when it got too dark to see. When they had nothing to report – no one matching Tom's description turned up in area hospitals or morgues – we left. I suppose that's the part for which Becca can't forgive me. But what could we do. Tom had money. Credit cards. No bodies had turned up. He knew where we were going. We figured he'd meet up with us if he wanted to.

We drove to Nogales.

"You think we should turn around?" Priest sipped his health juice concoction from a plastic cup. It smelled like sewage.

"And do what?"

Priest drank, and stared into the night.

We took I-20 through the panhandle to I-10, then followed smaller roads whenever we could. I drove, except for short breaks to stretch my legs and doze in the starlight.

It wasn't until Las Cruces and the first signs of daybreak that the question I'd been wanting to ask spilled out.

"What was it made you re-fund the project?"

Priest wedged behind the wheel. He looked at me long enough that I worried we'd leave the road. "It's the nature of science – of any-thing, really – that today's revelation will look foolish tomorrow. The key to getting anything done – to really making a breakthrough – is to believe enough to push past that." In his cloth hat, long sleeves and giant, wraparound sunglasses, Priest cut a ridiculous figure. Buddha as desert chauffeur. "Stem cell research was going lots of good places, but not where I wanted it to go. Everyone was all hot for the disease-specific possibilities. That's where the real science is headed." A smirk danced on his lips. "But that's the trouble with real science – it lacks vision."

The Las Vegas Café, like everyplace else in the world, had gone upscale. Red tablecloths. A disappointment that might keep us from going back, except that the *ropas* are so damn good. Smoky strings of beef, complex spices intermingled for so long they finish each other's sentences.

We kept a seat open at the table for Tom, the way you're supposed to for Elijah. We almost didn't feel guilty being there. Tom has tasted it. He'd understand. Besides, it seemed as likely as not he'd walk through the door any second.

"I know what you're thinking, Max." Priest's pink face enraptured. "But it's not that simple." The way he rolled the meat on his tongue could get him arrested in some midwestern states. "It's easy to blame me and my money. Cite its corrupting influence." He emitted little moans as he ate – okay, we both did – drawing wary glances from other patrons, who hadn't traveled twenty-seven hundred miles to be there. "But there's no such thing as pure science. Pure anything."

"Wait," I said, but it's hard to stop Priest when he's on a roll.

"I'll tell you what real science is. It's not white lab coats. It's the nutcases out in the wilderness willing to think crazy thoughts, then spend their lives trying to actualize them." He wiped his mouth with warm tortilla. "You want to know what I think, your friend isn't willing to do the hard work."

I didn't want to know what he thought. Didn't want to acknowledge any possibility that serious. "I thought you said aliens."

Priest grinned. My shallowness appeals to him. "Or, it could be aliens."

Across from us, a little girl, maybe three years old, dark curls, ate at a plate of beans while her father, under a straw cowboy hat, watched foot traffic pass by on the sidewalk.

"Not all of us get labs at Harvard or MIT," Priest said. "Some of us have to articulate our vision from the UMass Medical Center."

"You're wrong about Tom," I said, though I spoke more from my heart than from any developed theory.

Priest, head buried in his food, looked at me over the frames of his glasses. "We'll see."

I had to break the news to Becca, and that's when she broke my nose. The accumulated frustration. The homosexuality. The presence of Fillmore Priest, who sat the whole time in the car. The tainted research. Her brother's fading star. My nose became the target of her anger over all that, maybe more. And we'd driven straight back, thirty-four hours, to tell her.

It's been two weeks now. A short vacation, from one viewpoint. An eternity, from another. Becca is beside herself with worry and anger. She's stopped talking to me altogether. She doesn't feel I'm taking this as seriously as I should. But I don't know what to say to her. I recognize the ugly possibilities – Tom may be hurt or lost or killed; he may have that brain injury Becca fixates on, or have fallen prey to random violence from some West Texas whack job. But I have to be positive about this. I have to.

Priest and I talk daily. He's angry for other reasons. "Karate and vitamins and shit juice are only going to take me so far," he says. "Aging is killing us all. I need my scientist." There was a moment where Priest lost himself, believed that Tom had planned this, had signed on to the revitalized project only to run off with the money; to Priest's credit, he didn't believe this for long.

As for me, I'm convinced Tom is taking care of business.

Here's the thing. If we're going to believe anything in a world where people vanish, we need to leave room for mystery. Be willing to live with what we don't know. We don't know where Tom is. We can't know – despite Becca's insistence – if God is, or what God thinks. Priest can't know if he'll ever find the cure he seeks. And Tom can't know if he's conducting hard science, or simply tilting at windmills with all of his gifts, all of Priest's money, all of our hope. How do we live with that uncertainty. That's the question I hope Tom is asking, the work I trust he's doing, wherever he is.

Symbiosis

ϒ

IN THE DREAM, HIS DAUGHTER calls to him, in that exasperated teenage voice, not to worry. No visual, just her voice calling to him, that "stop treating me like a child" tone.

Then he is at the window, entranced by a small puddle of water on the unpainted sill, hearing only the squeak of her footsteps on rotting floorboards, aware not of concern for her safety as much as annoyance at her intrusion. He has warned her that the floorboards are old, not safe, and she has chosen to ignore him. They are, he and his daughter, in his wife's parents' old barn. In the dream, the barn is in the condition he first saw it. A husk, listing badly to the south, with missing slats where the sun breaks through at odd and extreme angles. There is a wooden ramp, with crosspieces for traction, that leads up to an old hay loft. There is no longer a roof. The barn is open to the sky, the elements. And though it is clearly the barn, in the dream he understands it to be his wife's parents' house, and it is as though Clark and his daughter are waiting there for the others to come home.

He is in the living room of the barn, transfixed by the puddle of water on the window sill. In the puddle is a reflection, the hint of an image he cannot make out, and he is focused on that puddle, that image, when his daughter's voice calls out not to worry. When her footsteps creaking on the floorboards distract him, which causes the image to fade. He is trying to block out the sound of her footsteps and push aside his annoyance, to conjure the image, when he hears the crack of splintering wood.

"Emily," he calls. The sun through a gap in the slats illumines the wall to his left, where now there is wallpaper. That fact only marginally registers, because he is aware that his daughter's foot or leg has broken through the floorboards and he is trying not to be annoyed, trying not to think *I told you - why can't you ever listen.*

"Emily."

Outside the window, tree branches shake.

He pushes away from the window and walks toward the back of the barn, behind the ramp, where the sound came from. He ducks his head under and around thick beams. Through the missing slats, bright sunlight alternates with deep shadow. It disorients him, and he walks slowly, carefully, floorboards giving under his own feet.

As he ducks under the ramp, cobwebbed wood brushes his hair and he moves to where her voice came from, steps through shadow and light to the back wall of the barn. There are broken floorboards where a foot, even an ankle might have gone through. But there is no Emily. He calls to her. Searches the barn, the surrounding yard, but in the dream she is no longer there. She is gone.

"Why the long face?"

Clark and Emily at the breakfast table, Thursday morning. November chill. Emily's head half buried in a bowl of Cheerios.

"Horse walks into a bar," she says.

"Very good," he says. He wears layers for biking. Bikes to work every day, all year. Emily finds this equal parts admirable and humiliating. "So why the long face?"

"Tired," she says through waves of black hair.

It is unusual for her to make a weekday appearance at breakfast. Usually there is no time. Usually she is hustled out the door by Lisa, the two of them in various stages of mother-daughter agitation.

"Up late studying?" He eats oatmeal that he makes, every morning. On weekends, she often – well, sometimes now – joins him.

Her head may have nodded. "Math test." She shovels cereal into her mouth. "I don't get it," she says. "At all." As a young child, Emily had hurled herself at the world as if she were trying to break through to something. An intensity she has less of now. Sometimes Clark wonders how that changed. Where it's gone.

Lisa is in the shower. The sound reaches them like soft rain.

"Did you call someone for help?"

"Called everyone. No one gets it."

"Why didn't you ask me?"

"*Please.*"

The math she's doing now is beyond him. He'll spend an hour on a problem, his only route into it tortured, circuitous. The solution will turn out to be far more direct. This disappointment dangles between them as her grade suffers.

"Put it on my bill," he says. He loves the unlikely things that connect them. The dumb jokes. The music – country twang and bluegrass.

"Duck walks into a bar," she says, automatic.

He worries about her posture. It seems to him she always eats bent over her food like someone's doddering grandmother.

"I had this horrible dream," she says.

"Yeah? What about?"

"Nothing," she says. "Don't do that. I hate when you do that."

"Do what?"

The bathroom door opens. Lisa's footsteps cross the hall.

"You get all interested." Emily spoons cereal. Chews. Speaks with her mouth half-full. "Like nightmares are really cool."

"Dreams are interesting." His oatmeal features bits of dried figs, apricots and blueberries. "What was terrible?"

"Nothing," she says. She pushes away from the table. "I had a hard time getting back to sleep is all."

"They're just dreams, honey. Movies in your brain. Entertainment."

"Right, Dad."

"Okay," he says. "Tell me. What was so terrible?"

"I gotta go," she says. "Mom will be on me any second." She gathers her bowl and spoon and water glass. "It creeped me out is all." Starts toward the kitchen. "You were there," she says, as if it were something from real – waking – experience and he should remember. "I hurt my leg at Grandpa's house."

ϒ

He has the dream again. Twice. In these revisitations, he notices additional detail. Although he can see branches quake outside the window in what would appear a strong wind, there is no sound of wind. In fact, no sound save his daughter's footsteps and her voice and his own breathing.

He notices furniture from Lisa's parents' house, wonders if that were there before. A green Victorian couch, plush and worn, dark wood and lots of curves. A cane rocker. A coffee table he cannot recollect in any detail. A framed family photograph, all five siblings, taken the summer before Lisa's oldest sister died.

Emily's steps on the floorboards. Clark's strained effort to see the image in the puddle. A yearning (is that new?) to see the image.

The barn is where Lisa played as a girl, with her sisters, sometimes her cousins. By the time he met her and saw the barn, it was a wreck, a kind of abstract sculpture.

In the dream, Emily's footsteps. Clark's puddle. Dark tree limbs. Something in the background. The footsteps, the creaking of the old boards, the knowledge that she is ignoring his advice, all inhibit his concentration. An animal at the edge of his vision, moving across the yard. He registers paws, brown fur. One of the dogs that wander the neighborhood. He wills into focus the image from the puddle. Then the crack of wood, and his irritation, and search for her. This time, when he gets back to where the hole is in the barn floor, he hears her voice call to him as if from a great distance, but he cannot locate the source or direction of the sound. Just her call, over and over, so distant he might be imagining it, or dreaming.

He badgers her into telling him about the dream, after he learns she's had it again. Saturday morning, over oatmeal.

"It's the house," he says.

"Yeah. Gramma and Grandpa's house."

"Not the barn."

"No, the house."

He'd spent the previous evening in the study, surrounded by maps of the Northern Territories. The lakes region of Canada. He is scheming a family canoe trip where they would get airlifted in for a week. Deposited. He pored over maps, both seeking the best area and working out in his head how he could present this so it would appeal to both Lisa and Emily.

Lisa works, devotedly. Administers a nonprofit foundation. Clark has mostly adjusted, his sense of family, what it means to be a parent. When Emily was five, Clark quit his high-tech job to teach high school. To spend more time with her. Have summers. Now, Lisa tells him he needs to push Emily away. Let her go.

He tells Emily he's had the same dream. "There's a sense of water, right?"

"Yeah, but no *actual* water," she says.

They explore the events. Other than the location, the dream is identical.

Her face flushes. "*Don't do that*," she says. "*Don't copy me.*"

"What does that mean?" he says. A radiator hisses and clanks. The house is old, and slow to warm. "Besides, I had it first."

"You don't know that."

She had gone out with friends. A movie. Until this year, she had been an enthusiast for family adventures.

They eat oatmeal. Drink water. She tells him details from her dream. Belligerently. Furniture. Stuff on the walls. Pictures. He doesn't have that. This seems to have been her intent. To claim ownership. Establish greater authenticity.

He moves her water glass away from the edge of the table, a reflex he can't always suppress. "So, in your version, where do you go?"

Her head hovers an inch over the bowl. She relocates her glass. Her hair smells of citrus, some new shampoo. "I don't know. My foot breaks through the floor, and everything's dark and scary, and then I wake up."

"Dark and scary how?"

"Dark. Scary."

"And then you wake up."

"Yeah, Dad." She hoists her spoon out of the oatmeal. Drops it back in. Glares at him. "Can we not talk about this anymore."

They eat oatmeal. Lisa asleep upstairs.

"Which foot?" he says.

"Left." An exasperated sigh. "You're supposed to be distant," she says. "Unapproachable. We're not even supposed to like each other."

He starts to protest but there is nothing to say.

"You've gotta admit, Dad. It's a little creepy."

Monday, she twists her ankle in volleyball practice. She tells him this on the phone, that evening. He's at his desk, at school, looking at a picture, he and Emily rock scrambling at Zion. Her pure joy of discovery. Life opening anew. He's going straight from school to a political meeting. Democratic party. Progressive stuff. The ankle's swelling. She will miss her game Wednesday, she tells him.

"Which ankle?" he says.

"Don't," she says, that determined edge in her voice. "I know what you're thinking. Just don't."

ϒ

It is not unusual for him to be both actor and observer in his dreams. A full participant, experiencing the emotions of whatever is happening, and simultaneously aware it is a dream – the stakes are not real. So there is a comfort level in allowing events to play out. He has always – since he was a kid – been intrigued rather than threatened by dreams, grateful for the windows into himself.

He has the barn dream again, though there is something grotesque about it this time – the stark way the light hits the walls, the disembodied sound of Emily's voice. This time, he is particularly aware of it as a dream, of himself as director, editor. He concentrates on blocking out her creaking footsteps so he can focus on the image in the puddle. He's not wearing his glasses, so he has to squint, and he's aware of hurrying, that his concentration, or the play of light, may change any moment. He is aware of soft edges, a grayness to things, like after a spring rain. He recognizes hair, wills it into focus. It's Emily's hair, and Emily, laying on grass, in an orange sun dress he and Lisa had brought her from their trip to Barcelona when she was twelve. There's a sound that's not footsteps and not Emily's voice. He's intent on the dress. Something on the dress. A stain. And her posture. He concentrates, and sees that she is not laying, she is sprawled, and the stain is blood, and it is not merely on her clothes, but on her arms, her face. And the sound he's hearing is a kind of animal chatter, a yip and yowl. He sees and hears this only for a moment before the crack of floorboards, quite loud, wakes him.

"What were you *thinking*?"
Clark tries to keep his voice level. To keep from escalating. He was waiting for her, leaning against the kitchen counter when she walked in the door.

"I was *thinking* I was hanging out with friends. I was *thinking* you weren't going to go all gestapo and check up on me." She stands just inside the door, jean jacket still on. Scarf. A lingering draft of chill air.

"For the record, Nina's parents called here looking for the two of you. I got worried when you weren't where you said you'd be."

"Well you shouldn't have."

"You were supposed to be at Nina's house. It was supposed to be just the three of you, just girls." His back to the sink. He is a natural barrier to her entry deeper into the house.

"What difference does it make? There was nothing going on. No drugs. No orgies. We were watching a movie, for God's sake."

"That's not the point. You lied to me."

"You wouldn't have let me go."

"You're not even hearing –" He stops himself. He makes a habit to resist ranting about what are simply developmental facts of life. "You're grounded."

"Fine." She faces dark windows, arms folded, making a point of not looking at him. Outside, it's Friday night.

"You don't want to know details? Boundaries? How long?"

"*Whatever.*"

He takes a deep breath. Feels undermined. He swallows back that frustration. Give her a chance. "Anything else you want to say?"

"No." She won't meet his eyes. Won't turn toward him. All he can see is hair and chin. He pushes away from the counter. Cold tile. Cold air. Toward the living room.

Her voice. Sharp. A blade. "Stop following me."

He turns. Puzzled.

The intensity of her stare unnerves him. "My dreams."

Emily home from school, Wednesday, a walking day. Her backpack deposited on the kitchen floor, so he has to step over it. This is not unusual, and he tries to mention it only when it especially bothers him.

He is sautéing red peppers to add to the pasta sauce he is making. He is making it without tomato chunks, even though he prefers it with tomato chunks, because Emily will not eat tomato chunks. Lisa has called in from the road, from traffic, on her way.

"Hey," he says, adjusting the flame under the peppers. "How was your day?"

"Okay." She forages the counter, finds some almonds. "Smells good."

"Mom's in traffic." On the right front burner, the sauce simmers and steams. "Wanna make a salad?"

A frown. "Not really." She chews almonds. Leans against the counter, so he will have to circumnavigate both her and her backpack. "I need to tell you something."

"Tell me while you make a salad."

"And I need you to not freak out."

Instant alert. "Did something happen?"

"*Dad.* I'm here, right? Just listen."

Clark concentrates on the peppers, the reassuring sizzle.

Emily retrieves a bag of greens from the refrigerator. "I'm walking through the arboretum, right, not the Peter's Hill part but the part before that, and I'm on the path along the brook, and it's really quiet, no one around, and it's just the beginning of dark, just a little shadow, and I get this weird sense like someone's following me."

Clark focuses on the peppers.

"But there isn't." Emily picks through the bag, avoiding the more bitter baby greens. "I look around, a couple times, and I don't see anyone. Then I'm getting close to the gate, you know, where you cross Weld Street, and I feel it again, and I look up, and there, on the other side of the brook, is this animal, walking along just ahead of me. I figure it's a dog, but there's no owner, no leash, and that funny walk." She jostles the salad bowl, gauging the minimum acceptable amount. "So it's a coyote."

Clark fixes his eyes on the peppers, his ears on his daughter's voice.

"And I stop when I see him, cause, you know he kinda takes me by surprise. And he stops, too. And we watch each other, like we're each checking the other out. And I kinda grin, cause it's like we're both figuring out what to do, if anything, or what this means, you know, and I swear when I grin at him he starts walking again, what do they call it that limping walk, loping, still watching me over his shoulder while I went out the gate." She holds almonds and watches him add the peppers to the sauce.

He wonders if she can see the tremble in his hand. He wonders if she is somehow messing with him, a strange variant of teenage insurgence.

"So that was last week sometime. And it happens, same area, again today." She watches him for a reaction.

He wills his face to reveal nothing. He folds peppers into sauce. He is on alert, but against what? There is no evident threat, no protocol. "It follows you – both times?" A coincidence, he tells himself.

"Yeah. But wait," Emily says. "Here's the creepy part."

Clark feels short of breath. "Yeah?"

"Remember, you need to not freak out."

"*Okay.*"

"So this thing, with the coyote," she says. "I've had that *exact* dream."

He stirs sauce. He counts silently to thirty. He can't think.

She watches him. Twirls her hair. "Nature encounter, right? Animal protector?"

"That's right," he says. He stirs sauce. Sniffs it.

"What?" she says.

He won't look at her.

"*What?*" She twirls her hair. The kitchen warm with cooking. She has shot up nearly three inches in the last year. Some days he barely recognizes her. "*Shit*," she says. "You had it, too."

He shakes his head. Flushed. Woozy. "No. I didn't."

"You're lying," she says. "*You had the dream.*"

"Go wash up for dinner."

"You had the dream."

He nods grudgingly. He feels lost. Out of his depth. "A version of it."

Her finger presses hard against the counter. Her cheeks flush red. "Why are you *doing* this to me. Stop it, Dad. *Leave me alone.*"

She stomps to her room.

After dinner, he says in his most casual voice, "I'm thinking I should meet you after school on Wednesdays. We can take the T together."

Emily rolls her eyes. "Do you have any idea how that would look?"

Lisa in the kitchen, cleaning dishes.

"Worse than grounding, that's how." Emily traces with her finger on the table.

The clink of plates from the next room.

A memory follows him to his study, where he tweaks plans for the Canada canoe trip. Then later into bed, into restless sleep. Emily at four, his family's Labor Day party on the quarry in Rockport. The water clear, bottomless. His sister claims to have touched. He has never managed it. Clark on the deck, absorbing sun. The smell of grilled meat. He has told Emily no swimming. Too dangerous. Languid end-of-summer day. Something flickered behind his eyelids, a shadow or parental sixth sense. His eyes opened to see Emily fly off the dock, into the water and down. A corona of black hair lingering briefly at the surface. The longest seconds of his life to react. Respond. Dive.

He feels that way now. A loss of equilibrium. An inadequacy. He wonders what forces are at work here. But he is not someone who believes one person can control, or even influence, another's dream. Not someone who believes dreams follow us into waking life.

"Where you off to?" Emily in her bedroom, at her desk, her computer. Lisa is at yoga, Clark has his biking gear on. Backpack at his feet. Outside, it's dark and cold.

"Ward meeting."

"Don't ride. Please." She has her scarf wrapped loose around her throat. Hair pulled back. She is reflected in the skylight above her desk.

"Will it embarrass you?"

"Dad, the streets froze. There's ice. People don't ride in that. Not sane ones."

"All kinds of people do. All year."

"Why can't you take the bus? The car? For once."

"Will power."

"You are *so* strange."

"You used to brag on that."

"Yeah, well. I also used to like bluegrass." A wind draws both their eyes to the skylight, a pattern of ice at its perimeter. "Which losing cause is this?"

"Governor. We can win this one."

"Keep telling yourself that." She says this with a smile. She flips the long end of her scarf over her right shoulder, gets up and kisses his cheek. "Be careful out there," she says.

He shoulders his backpack, her voice soft behind him.

"This is something that happens, right?" she asks him. "I mean, it's normal? This dream thing."

They have always talked about the importance of honesty. Telling each other the truth. "I don't know." He puts his helmet on. He is a poster boy for safe riding. "Weird stuff happens sometimes. Let's try to not make more of it than it is."

She drinks from a water glass at the edge of her desk. A ring has worn itself into the wood. "I mean it's developmental or something, right?" She kneads the end of the scarf in her fingers. "And it's gonna be okay?"

"Yeah, kiddo." He tries to think of something both truthful and reassuring. "Nothing to worry about. Don't stay up too late."

Υ

She is in the kitchen of their house, Emily is, and it's sunny like in the other dream, light streaming in the south windows, and he is in the study looking at maps of the Northern Territories, scheming the canoe trip. The sun warms his left shoulder and he soaks that in because the rest of the house is so cold. He can see his breath, little puffs of vapor as he pores over the map. Emily rustling in the kitchen. Foraging. Cupboards opening, closing. On the map, Canada is yellow. The border between Manitoba and Saskatchewan a snaking red line. Then breaking glass, and her voice calling out – *Dad.*

Dad. I broke a glass.

On the map, the pale green rectangle of North Dakota. *It's okay,* he says. *Just clean it up.* Michigan a purple mitten. He has always wanted to visit Saskatchewan. His goal for the trip is incidental encounters with moose.

A pause, then Emily's voice. *I need help.*

He leaves the map, pulls his shoulder out of the warm sun and into the kitchen where she clutches the broken glass in her hand. A jagged edge has cut into her wrist. Blood drips onto the floor. The sleeve of her sweater. How teenagers can be so oblivious. Though he walks toward her, he gets no closer than a few feet. Just beyond arm's reach. He notices this, but doesn't ponder it. He is focused on the glass cutting into her wrist, her fingers where she clutches it. Red blood against white cotton.

Emily, he says softly. *Put the glass down. You're hurting yourself.* She looks puzzled, as if she can't hear what he's saying, or doesn't recognize him. He says it louder, takes a few steps toward her but the distance between them in the kitchen remains the same. *Emily*, he says. *Your fingers.* And he mimes the gesture, unfolding the fingers of his one hand with the fingers of his other. *Let go.* It is as if she is trying to listen to him, trying to understand what he asks. And as she tries, her hand clutching the glass squeezes tighter from the effort, and he can't stop saying *Let go* and she can't stop looking at him and squeezing, trying to understand or trying to ignore and the blood runs down her forearm and into a growing puddle on the tile floor.

Let go.

Then, as if considering his request, his urging, she takes the hand clutching the glass and scratches at the side of her face. The jagged part of the glass cuts into her cheek and then her neck and blood drips across her collarbone and down into her sweater and onto the floor.

And he calls out to her to stop, loud now, and reaches for her hand which is just beyond his grasp, and she chuckles, as if he is mimicking her teenage tendency to drama. As if she found that amusing.

Acknowledgements

No long face here. Just gratitude.

Some of those it goes out to: the editors and publications that have
embraced my work and supported me along the way, especially Rusty
Barnes, Ilena Silverman and Adrienne Miller—outstanding editors
and advocates, all. Mentors Gene Garber, Judy Johnson, Don Schatz.
All those who have walked this with me, especially Jeff, John, Paul,
Jehanne, Ginny, DDoyle, Susan, Deb, Lisa, Fred, Lori, Scott. Jenna
and Ralph, for the kind words and heartfelt support. Team Swank,
my tribe, my fellow explorers. Grub Street, my writing home. Chau-
tauqua Summer Writers Institute, Sitio Serra de Estrella and Dorland
Mountain Arts Colony, for supporting the cause. Laura Davidson,
for your inspiring art and for making collaboration fun. God bless
Rhythm & Muse. Finally, Jan Ramjerdi, whose committed and
relentless editing has made this a better book, and me a better writer;
and Barb and Megan, who make every day good.

About the Author

RON MacLEAN is a recipient of the Frederick Exley Award for Short Fiction, and a recurring Pushcart Prize nominee. His novel *Blue Winnetka Skies* was published in 2004. He lives in Boston with his family.

About Swank Books

SWANK BOOKS is a collaborative press founded in 2002 and committed to the advancement of independent fiction. Visit us on the web at www.swankbooks.com.